EVERYTHING
BEAUTIFUL

Also by Simmone Howell

Notes from the Teenage Underground

EVERYTHING BEAUTIFUL

SIMMONE HOWELL

BLOOMSBURY

LONDON BERLIN NEW YORK

Bloomsbury Publishing, London, Berlin and New York

First published in Great Britain in 2009 by Bloomsbury Publishing Plc,
36 Soho Square, London, W1D 3QY

First published in 2008 by Pan Macmillan Australia Limited

Lines from *With Mercy for the Greedy*
Reprinted by permission of SII/Sterling Lord Literistic, Inc.
Copyright by Anne Sexton

Every effort has been made to contact copyright holders of material reproduced
in this book. Any person or organisation that may have been overlooked
should contact the publisher.

A CIP catalogue record of this book is available from the British Library

ISBN 978 0 7475 9785 8

FSC
Mixed Sources
Product group from well-managed
forests and other controlled sources
Cert no. SGS-COC-2061
www.fsc.org
© 1996 Forest Stewardship Council

The paper this book is printed on is certified independently in accordance with the
rules of the FSC. It is ancient-forest friendly. The printer holds chain of custody.

Printed and bound in Great Britain by Clays Ltd, St Ives Plc

10 9 8 7 6 5 4 3 2 1

www.bloomsbury.com/GabrielleZevin

For my parents, who let me ask all the questions

ON THE FIFTH DAY

OUTLAWS

I am the maniac behind the wheel of a stolen dune buggy. Dylan Luck is at my side. We are tearing up the desert, searching for proof of God. My driving experience amounts to a few stuttering laps of the Safeway car park. *That* was supervised – Dad blanching and clutching his seatbelt. *This* is something else; something beginning with Freedom.

While the rest of the campers were singing their thirty-fifth Bottle of Beer down the highway, Dylan and I made our escape. We had petrol siphoned from the counsellors' cars. We had supplies – snacks and Band-Aids and bottled water – all hauled to Fraser's garage where Delilah was waiting under a dirty tarp. Delilah started life as a 1967 VW Beetle, but she's had 'work' – her chassis shortened, her body stripped back to a shell. She has bucket seats and sand tyres and a 'demi' windshield that sits like reading glasses on her pert bonnet. We didn't build her, but we did christen her – after some dispute.

'It has to be a girl's name,' Dylan said. 'Cars and ships always have girls' names. It's a macho-sexist-transport thing.'

'What do you call your wheelchair?'

He thought about this, then smiled. 'My Bitch.'

It feels like we're flying down the corrugated track. Dust swirls behind us like a cowgirl's wedding train. There's nothing like going so fast you have to squint; so fast your cheeks wobble, and the wind ploughs your hair and judders in your ears like a tattooist's drill. Delilah has no floor, just pedals sticking up. My feet stay on them waiting to stomp. Clutch in – gas out. I do the dune buggy two-step, wild and gleeful. Shrieks fly out of my mouth like bats.

Dylan roars too, mocking Neville, our twee camp counsellor – 'I feel so ALIVE!'

He rattles his chair, which is folded and fixed to a bar in front of his knees. In the corner of my eye I can see the chair's Playboy mudflaps. They're homemade and have a wonky charm – like their maker. Five days ago, when I first saw Dylan, I felt sorry for him. I never thought he'd make me laugh so hard or act so crazy. First impressions are arse.

As we zoom along the fire road I think about topography. Twenty thousand years ago the Little Desert was under sea. I close my eyes for the briefest of seconds and see ridges and reefs and whirlpools. Then: CRACK! The world tilts and Delilah starts to skid. She's lost a wheel, and I'm losing my footing. There is swerving and swearing and shuddering and then there is the tree – one of those fat red mallee bastards that a week ago I wouldn't have known the name of. We hit the trunk on my side. I lurch into the steering wheel. Time stops. When I fall back against the vinyl, my face feels stiff; my arm hurts something ferocious. Dylan has hardly moved. He had the chair as his buffer – plus he has superior upper body strength. Not that you'd know it to look at him – his chest is more crushed tinnie than buff six-pack.

Our first reaction is to look at each other and baulk. Then we laugh.

I say, 'Are we dead?'

Dylan checks his legs. He lifts each one and lets it drop down. 'If this is Heaven I want a refund.' For Dylan, Heaven is where his legs work. I don't know what Heaven is for me – unless it's us, here, this.

I hear something. It sounds like the first cart climbing a roller coaster, or a parrot pecking at a bush apple. But the noise is just my teeth chattering.

'Are you okay?' Dylan says. 'Your head – '

I touch my forehead. When I bring my hand back, my fingers are wet with blood. 'Oh.' I check myself in the side mirror. I have a cut, dead centre – a perfect, red spot.

'You look like one of the Manson girls,' Dylan studies me. 'I always thought you'd look cute with a third eye.'

I'm too fuzzy to summon a comeback. I try to laugh and feel myself slip a little in the seat.

Dylan brushes his thumb across my brow. I press my head into his hand.

'It's okay,' he says stroking my hair. I stay down. I feel woozy, flooded. I have an insane urge to tell him that I love him. I want to say that if we really are dead it would be sad in a way, but in another way it would be the perfect outlaw end. I picture the sand turning into sea again, rising and rising, folding over us and preserving us forever. But talking takes too much effort. So I close my eyes. The sky stays blue behind them and there are no clouds for the longest time.

IN THE BEGINNING

THE PALACE OF SUCKDOM

The first sign we were entering the Palace of Suckdom came as we passed under the wooden arches. They had a shipwrecked look and were etched with this: *He Hath Made Everything Beautiful In His Time.*

'There's a challenge.' Dad winked at me in the rear-view mirror. 'Someone's got their work cut out for them.'

'Ha, ha.' I made a face. It was high noon. Outside the window was a wilderness of dust.

'Ron!' Norma cried. She turned to me, 'Don't listen to him, pet. You're gorgeous.' Then she trilled, 'And we're *here*! Are you excited?'

'I'm so excited I need the toilet.'

'Riley.' Dad's voice was like a jab in the ribs.

'What?'

'You know.' He mouthed 'Be Nice'. Be Nice to Norma – that old refrain. Well I didn't want to be nice. He couldn't banish me and still expect sunshine smiles. 'Here' was Spirit Ranch Holiday Camp. The website boasted '*an oasis of fun and learning on the edge of the Little Desert: From*

Pomponderoo Hill to the southern crater – nowhere is God's work more in evidence.' From where I was sitting it looked like a horror movie set: closed up and quiet – too quiet. I wasn't excited. I was banished. The closest town was called Nhill – and that's exactly where I set my expectation levels.

It had been a long drive, made longer by Norma's New Age soundtrack – fern gullies, waterfalls, the tranquil sounds of whale sex. I couldn't stop staring at Norma's hand planted on Dad's thigh. Traveller's hand. Mum used to do that. But Mum's hand was a salve; Norma's was like a falconer's mitt.

My mother, Lilith Maree Rose, died two years ago, when I was fourteen. Of all of the facts of my life, this was the one that wouldn't change. If I ever chanced to forget about the Mum-shaped hole in my life, the grief would come back like a Chinese burn on my heart. It was Cancer – fast and ugly – and it left Dad and I gasping for air. *Pain ends* – if you believe the grief guides. Apparently visualisation helps – *close your eyes, imagine you see your loved one laughing, open your eyes. Breathe*. Cue me: sweet sixteen and still gasping. I felt incomplete, cut up and I couldn't talk about it. Insert life change here.

Six months after Mum died, Dad moved us back to the 'burb where he grew up. He had all his old friends and I made precisely one: Chloe Benson. Dad started going to church again and not just on Sundays – he got *involved*. It was months of church-activity craziness. He even auditioned for *Moses – The Musical*. Dad is a terrible singer. His breathing is all over the place. He sings like someone's chasing him – and it turns out someone was. Norma. Her name is onomatopoeic which means she looks like she sounds – she's all soft and droopy-drawly, and she's kind. I didn't want her to be kind.

When term ended Dad sat me down to tell me that he and Norma were 'pretty serious'. And even though the rest of me was numb I still managed a smart mouth because that's my best defence. I said, '*Pretty* serious? *Pretty?* A qualifier is like a seed of doubt.' Dad squeezed my hand and that squeeze cut the qualifier out.

My smart mouth is one defence; my weight is another. I am Chubby Con Carne, eighty-two kilos and rising. The whole Norma Trauma kit came with free counselling. 'Do you think, Riley, that your weight is the moat around the real you?' Or, 'Would you say, Riley, that you only feel good when you're being bad?'

All year I'd been hurtling towards catastrophe. There was the thing with the bucket bong, my almost failing mid-terms, my schizo MO – hugging Dad one day, railing at him the next – but the tipping point was when a group of us broke into the local pool for a spot of night-swimming. Your honour, I admit it. We were drunk on vodka jellies. My mascara had run in Vampira streaks down my face, which was delirious-happy because *I was just about to kiss Ben Sebatini!* He of the inky hair and that smile that made me steady myself against stair-rails. I still can't believe that for nine hot minutes – until the cops busted in and ripped us asunder – the boy was mine.

Dad picked me up at the station and we drove home in

silence. In the driveway, he killed the lights, hung his head and said, 'Riley, Riley, Riley.'

I went, 'What's up, Mr Potato-head?' but he didn't laugh like usual.

'You don't take anything seriously.' His voice was so quiet I had to hunch to hear it. 'You don't seem to understand that there are consequences in life. You're messing up. And I don't know what to do with you.'

'I'm sure Norma has a few ideas,' I said under my breath.

That night I bent my ear to the ducted heating vent and listened to Dad and Norma plot my course. They had their first holiday coming up. A winsome week of B&Bs and cellar doors. I was supposed to stay at Chloe's but there was no way Dad was going to let that fly now. Norma suggested Spirit Ranch. A friend of a friend from the parish had sent her daughter there and she'd come back Saved. She'd gone from shaving her eyebrows to reading *The Sisterhood of the Travelling Pants*. Camp was booked solid but Norma was connected. All it would take was a phone call.

Dad wavered. 'I guess it would get her away from Chloe . . .'

'But?' Norma prodded.

'I don't want her to feel like I'm dumping her.'

'Ron. You're too sensitive.'

'I don't know . . .'

'Honey, you have to take something for yourself here. It's like teaching a baby to swim. You have to just throw them in. Once they get over the shock, they love it.'

Norma's never had a baby. I know this for a fact.

*

The next day I debriefed Chloe.

'Talk about pussy-whipped!' she crowed.

'Norma doesn't have a "pussy",' I popped the 'p'. 'More like an old box with creaky hinges.'

Chloe and I creaked at each other and then fell apart laughing.

Chloe's like an ancient Vegas pole-dancer trapped in the body of a sixteen-year-old. She has lax parents, a disposable income and a serious guy habit. My first sleepover at her house featured her then-boyfriend Matt, his friend Andy, and a bottle of Jägermeister. The morning after she said, 'You know, when you're wanking a guy, sometimes it helps if you spit on your hand.' Everyone at school was scared of Chloe, but I, as her protégé, was safe. I liked her bent wisdom, but I couldn't picture us after high school – sharing a flat, or going to uni or having any adventures that didn't include body-shots and bohunks.

We took turns punching her faux-fur pillow.

'Wahh,' she cried. 'You're going to miss Ben Sebatini's party.'

'I know – it's like every time I get close, the cruel hand of fate rips up the set.' I hung my head. 'And I'm left on the stage . . . alone and forsaken.'

'The cruel hand of fate is a bitch.'

I showed her the Spirit Ranch brochure.

Chloe's eyes glittered. 'Will there be nuns? Make sure you take photos. I want to see wimples and control pants. Just think of all that dag couture . . .'

'I'm not allowed to bring my phone.'

'What?'

'No phones, no gadgets.' I sighed. 'It's totally Mormonic.'

Chloe laughed.

'Don't,' I said. 'This is Terminal.'

'My friend, my friend . . .' She pressed the pillow to my face and then flung it on the floor. 'I think you're fucked.' She uncurled her long, brown legs and stood up. She did one of her power yoga poses – the tree – closing her eyes and breathing out through her nostrils, short, fast and furious. Then she opened her eyes and declared, 'I'm going to get you out of this.'

'How?'

'Leave it with me.'

The day before I left for camp, I cut my hair. One side fell in ascending steps down my face, the other was straight, shoulder-length, civilian. Then I dyed it Ultra Violet.

I decided I would only pack frivolous things: eyelash curlers and costume jewellery and little jars of antipasto. If I had to go to Christian camp then I would go as a plague. I would be more like Chloe: outrageous and obnoxious – call me a plus-size glass of sin! It wasn't until Melbourne was wavering behind us like a bad watercolour that reality hit. As the kilometres ticked I sank in my seat and practised holding my breath. On a silo just past Horsham someone had painted an escape button. ESC – ten feet high against a concrete sky. I almost asked Dad to stop the car so I could press it.

ON THE FIRST DAY

SAFE FUN

Counsellor Neville's office was small and smelled like coffee and leftovers. For the first few seconds after our introduction he ignored us, and shifted papers around his messy desk. I kept quiet. The chair I was sitting in squeaked if I even breathed. Dad and Norma sat either side of me, like henchmen. Finally Counsellor Neville looked up and blinked at me. I blinked back. He was thirty-something, neat, and nothing much to look at until you saw his glass eye, then he took on a creepy character actor aspect: he's the guy with the sissy laugh and the knife taped to his ankle. He was wearing the standard shirt-tucked-into-jeans-and-'bonkers'-tie combo. On his pen pocket a badge proclaimed *God is Awesome* in bubble writing.

'Riley Rose.' He crossed off my name, my stupid name that sounds made-up or back-to-front, or like something I'm definitely not: Riley Rose – Romance Novelist. Riley Rose – Yodelling Cowgirl. Try Riley Rose – Defective Daughter. Unhappy Camper. Castaway. I stared at my palms like an acid kid, counting the cracks in my love-line while Neville rattled off the contents of my Spirit Ranch 'goody bag': 'One guidebook featuring map, information, your all-important schedule, and a little local history. One nametag – ' He tossed me a reddish button. My name was written on it in a primitive hand, underlined by a yellow feather. I turned the button over, accidentally puncturing my finger on the pin. There was no way I was going to wear it. In the first place it was hideous, and in the second, my top was only made out of finest fishnet. Like I would violate it with that monstrosity.

Neville smiled wetly. 'Roslyn made them, out of resin I believe. Roslyn is our art-life-spirit counsellor – she'll explain about the feather at Orientation. We'd like you to wear your nametag the first day or so, until you get to know your group.' He went back to the bag. 'One Spirit Ranch pen. Test it please – last year's lot were faulty.'

I scribbled on the cover of the guidebook, dumbly, dutifully. It was already too hot. Neville's air-conditioner was all noise and no action. I checked the sweat patch under his arm. Since I'd been there it had grown in size from a twenty-cent piece to a small pikelet.

'Sunscreen. Water bottle. Insect repellent. Visor.' Neville was winding up. 'You're in cabin three with Fleur and Sarita. Orientation is at four, then activities, then dinner. It's all on your schedule.'

Norma leaned forwards. 'Sarita . . . that's an interesting name. Is that Indian?'

Neville nodded.

My hand was still moving over the page. I was drawing thick black psychotic lines. Neville reached forward and held the end of my pen. 'I think it works.' Then he drum-rolled the desk and showed me his teeth. 'Welcome to Spirit Ranch Holiday Camp. Any questions?'

My brain had gone fuzzy. I shifted and the seat squeaked. My pants were riding up my bum. My top was too tight. 'There's been a mistake,' I blurted. 'I'm an atheist, agnostic, irreligious.' I couldn't remember the right word, but what I meant was this: *I'm different. I don't belong here.* Dad cleared his throat and Norma's smile went rictus. Neville's eye wobbled a bit but he kept his cool.

'Riley, Spirit Ranch is for everyone. Being "Christian" isn't a requirement. We just ask for an open mind, and hope you'll get involved, make some friends, learn some new skills, and most importantly, have fun.'

'*Safe* fun,' Norma added.

Neville had both hands in the air, fingers suspended in air quotes. Air quotes are something I've seen adults do when they're trying to 'relate'. They use 'teen argot' but they always bend uncomfortably when they're at it because they know damn well their youth is 'spent'. And maybe they don't like how they spent it, so every time they see a 'young person' they get crabby and offended or smarmy and patronising.

I could feel sweat collecting in all my corners. I made a half-turn, a whole plea. 'Dad?' He gave Norma the nod and she ushered me outside. We sat on a picnic bench in silence. A scenario unfolded in my head: Dad was in there apologising to Neville for wasting his time. He'd had a sudden flash of clarity. Spirit Ranch was not the place for his daughter. He was going to take me home, and leave Norma behind.

We'd go back to our house full of books and baking trays and never speak of this again.

'So, how do you like it?' Norma asked.

I stared at her. She was so nice, and earnest and *involved*. She had a hundred projects and now she was making one out of me. I said, 'You know, Dad and I used to have fun on our holidays. *Actually.*'

Norma stared back and for the first time I saw shades of steel. 'Do you think your father's been having *fun*? You've put him through the wringer, pet. The only way he'll get a holiday is if you're not in it.' She patted her hair and switched on a smile as Dad shambled out the door towards us.

'I'm not staying,' I told him.

'Come on, Potato-head.' He put his arm around my shoulder like he always does when he's just about to disappoint me. 'Give it a chance. They've got canoeing . . . and a flying fox.'

'Gee, that's great. Because I *so adore* physical activity.'

'Just take it at your own pace,' Norma advised me.

'You might even make some friends,' Dad coaxed.

'As if I'd want to make friends with the people here.'

I stirred the dust with my shoe, thinking last holidays we had take-away every night. Last holidays is a country I can never go back to.

'If you leave me here I'll run away,' I declared.

'Riley,' Dad said. 'It's seven days. It won't kill you.'

'I don't even believe in God!'

'You're sixteen. You don't know what you believe in.'

'Bullshit!' I grabbed my suitcase out of his hand and

stomped off across the quadrangle. In my head I made a list; by the time I'd reached my cabin it had become a manifesto:

I believe in Chloe and chocolate.
I believe the best part is always before.
I believe that most girls are shifty and most guys are dumb.
I believe the more you spill, the less you are.
I don't believe in life after death or diuretics or happy endings.
I don't believe anything good can come from this.

BLACK BALL

Inside cabin three there was a bunk and a single bed. The single was in prime position by the window but somebody had already claimed it, using her suitcase as a stake. I peeked in and saw polythene-packed clothes. Just what I needed, an OCD girl, the kind who carried antiseptic hand gel and can only have one type of food on her fork at a time. I moved the suitcase to the floor and lay on the bed in coffin-pose. Then I sat up and weighed Chloe's goodbye present in my hand. It felt like a book. It was probably a Bible. *Nice one, Chloe.* 'Don't open it until you get there,' she'd said. I tore through the wrapping paper. Sure enough it was an old hardback, *Utopia* by Sir Thomas More. The cover was brown cloth and faded. Inside, the print was large and there were old-fashioned illustrations and maps.

Chloe had left a note:

My friend, my friend. This is what you call a bunker book. It's big and intimidating and multi-purpose. You can use it as a weapon or you can cut a hole in it and stash life's little essentials: you know, poker chips, acid tabs . . . But before you do any of that I recommend that you turn to page 67. And then come back.

I turned to page sixty-seven. An envelope fell out. I opened it. It was a bus ticket. From Nhill to Melbourne, leaving Wednesday – at 10.30 pm.

This is important. The bus only goes once a week but it'll get you home in time for Ben Seb's. I'll pick you up at the station, Thursday am. My folks are away so we can do whatever. We can order pizza and bang the delivery boy. It'll be cool. Re: the bus. My advice is to sit next to a lady, and if some gross farmer tries to pick you up, pretend to be deaf. In the meantime, do me proud, make trouble and always remember that Jesus Loves You.
    Chloe

I stared at the ticket for a long time, a smile growing on my face. In the background I could hear a fly trapped behind the window screen. I listened to its blind buzz until I couldn't stand it anymore. Then I pulled the screen open and, using my bunker book, put the fly out of its misery. I was going home! I was going to get Ben Sebatini! The plan wasn't foolproof. Dad and Norma would find out eventually. I'd have to answer some sticky questions and I'd probably be grounded until menopause but anything was better than staying here.

I lifted a corner of the blind. The quadrangle was filling up with campers. They wore bright colours. They seemed to know each other. There were miles of smiles and rampant hugging. An aerial view would look like a snooker game on brown baize – the coloured balls dispersed, came together, and dispersed again. I could see how the game was going to play out. I was going to be the black ball.

Two girls had broken from the pack and were walking towards cabin three. This had to be Fleur and Sarita – my roomies. I could tell everything I needed to know just by looking at them. Fleur was the Valkyrie. Her face was just a little too sharp to be beautiful. The end of her nose pointed up piggishly. She had dancer's legs and caramel-coloured hair. The suitcase was hers for sure. Sarita was tiny, doll-like. She was wearing sensible shorts and the Spirit Ranch sun visor. Tragic! Under it, two plaits thick as jungle vines hung halfway down her back. Fleur was doing most of the talking – it looked like she was giving instructions. Sarita said something. Fleur stopped and smacked her on the arm.

'No way!' Her mouth flapped open, unhinged. 'Who told you?'

They had stopped just outside the door. I ducked down from the window.

Sarita's voice trembled with Bollywood gravitas. 'I saw him in the car park, with his mother. She was crying. I heard he jumped sixteen floors.'

'Oh God. This is awful.' Fleur moaned. There was silence,

then she said harshly, 'What? Why are you looking at me like that?'

'I'm not looking . . . like anything.'

'You better not,' Fleur warned. She pushed the door open to reveal: one Riley Rose, lounging on the single bed in a pose that I hoped was reminiscent of a 1950s burlesque star. Hands behind head, fingers underlining the brim of my floppy black hat, everything else out and proud, legs crossed at the ankles.

'Hola.' I fluttered my silver-painted fingertips.

Fleur groaned. 'Great.' She turned to Sarita. 'I thought it was going to be just us two.'

Sarita looked grave. 'You're not Poppy.'

Fleur said, 'Dumb-head! I told you. Poppy's got glandular.' She circled her throat. 'Her glands swelled up to here. She looked like one of those frogs that carry their babies in their mouths. She couldn't leave the house.'

They both stared at me. Fleur looked annoyed. Sarita looked worried. She seemed to be staring at my chest, so I pushed my boobs together with my hands. 'Pretty impressive, huh?'

Sarita's face went a deep shade of red.

'She was looking for your *name*tag.' Fleur's lip curled. 'Who *are* you?'

I flopped my hand for her to kiss. 'Riley Rose. Charmed. *Utterly.*'

'Oh.' She ignored my hand, scowling. 'Where's my stuff?'

'I relocated it.' I sighed. 'I can't possibly sleep in a bunk. I get claustrophobia. And vertigo.' Silence followed so I decided to keep spinning. 'Also, I sleepwalk – just so you know. It can be a bit of a shock to the uninitiated because I like to sleep *au naturel*.'

'Are you French?' Sarita asked.

'*Mais non*. But I speak several languages. *Un peu*. Conversational. When one travels, one cannot help but pick up some of the vernacular.'

Fleur snorted. Something about the set of her face made me vow right there and then to never tell her the truth about anything. She huffed past me, picked up her case from the floor and began to unpack on the bottom bunk.

'Well, come on,' she snapped at Sarita. 'Help me.'

Fleur started taking items of clothing out of plastic bags. She passed them to Sarita who looked at each piece reverently before re-folding it and placing it in Fleur's chest of drawers.

'So what do you do for fun around here?' I drawled.

Sarita smiled. 'There is always plenty to do. We have games. There's a talent show on the last day.'

'You never go in the talent show.' Fleur reminded her.

'It is true. I have no talent,' Sarita sighed. 'There's the campfire . . . lots of singing. Last year we went into the desert – '

'Did you find yourself?' I asked.

'Oh. I – ' Sarita looked at Fleur, flummoxed.

'She's teasing you,' Fleur said.

'I'm not much for nature,' I said with a shrug. 'I'm a city girl. Sophisticated, you know.'

'Oh well,' Fleur said testily. 'Don't expect to have much fun here then.'

'I don't.'

There was a moment of dead air. Fleur turned back to her suitcase. Sarita licked her lips and nodded at me and whispered, 'I am enamoured of your hat.'

'Oh!' I was surprised but I made a quick recovery. 'It's from Barcelona,' I lied, careful to pronounce the 'c' as 'th'.

Sarita was looking at me like I had the answer to everything. The intensity of her stare made me want to laugh. And then it made me nervous. I didn't want to be anyone's answer.

Fleur suddenly asked, 'How much do you weigh?'

In my mind's eye I punched her. It happened in beautiful slow motion. My fist hit her jaw. Her flesh wobbled, her mouth opened, spit came out, and a bit of blood, a couple of teeth. Mum used to say that anyone who used your appearance as ammo was the worst kind of bully – weak and unimaginative. She would have had Fleur pegged. I heard her in my ear. *If that's the best she can do, then you've already won.*

'I need air,' I decided. 'Please – don't go through my things. Certain items may offend.' I stood up and flung my bag over my shoulder, and gave Fleur a hard stare. 'And FYI. I weigh eighty-two kilos and I don't give a fuck.'

SPIRIT RANCH HOLIDAY CAMP SCHEDULE

NB: This schedule is subject to change

7 am – Showers

8 am – Breakfast

All meals are communal. If you have any special dietary requirements please see Roslyn.

9 am–12 pm – Activity

Physical challenges. All in. Good Sportsmanship is a definite prerequisite. If you have any health concerns please see Roslyn.

12 pm–1 pm – The Word

Interactive Bible-based activities and discussion. You will each have your turn to speak. Please give other speakers your attention and respect.

1 pm – Lunch

2 pm–5 pm – Activity

5 pm–6 pm – Free Time

Campers are encouraged to access the Recreation Room facilities for this period.

6 pm – Dinner

7 pm–10 pm – Indoor Activity

Film nights, reading, theatre sports in the Recreation Room. Campers may retire to their cabins for quiet time.

11 pm – Lights Out

Lights Out will be strictly enforced.

If you have any questions at any time, please see a counsellor or Youth Leader.

Peace, Love and Jesus,
The Spirit Ranch Team

A Rare Bird

I sat on a picnic bench and speed-read my camp program.
On the cover happy campers formed a human pyramid on
a green expanse but as the newspapers kept saying, we were
in the middle of a drought. There was no lawn now, the area
matched its name: 'the plain'. The office, mess hall, recreation
room and counsellors' annexe were at one end of the plain
and the shower block was at the other. The cabins were lined
up either side like boxcars. They were squat, wood and
stucco. Each had an Aboriginal 'motif' painted on the door.
Mostly fish – all of them trying to swim home.

In his introduction, Neville wrote that the Little Desert
used to be a sea, and then after the sea dried up it became
home to the Wotjobaluk people. For 5000 years they sourced
food and dipped in the soaks. Then the European settlers
came. They tried to farm the land, but you can't get wheat
out of sand. Whatever they planted dried up and disappeared. Ossification. That's what it's called. I looked
around. My throat felt dry, my eyes itchy. If I wasn't careful
it would happen to me. I sat for a minute mustering up

delirium and then I started to run. I was barefoot, tripping bindies. My stretchy top kept riding above my jelly-belly but I didn't care. I had the sensation that everything on me was wobbling. Everything. *There's too much of me*, I thought. *I'm Too Much!* And this made me giggle and run even faster. I was out of my element at Christian camp. I was a rare bird, the mysterious maniac loon. 'Koo-Koo-KA-KA-KA!' I called out to a pale, speccy kid standing by the bubbler. 'AaaaiiiiEEEEEE!' I shrieked and flapped my wings and pretended to fly.

I stopped at the toilet block. From inside came the sound of water blasting, followed by a shriek. I padded in, liking the cool cement on my toes. All the shower doors were open but one. I stood outside it for half a second, then pushed. Three girls in the ten-to-twelve bracket – psycho-tweenies – were huddled over a girl who was lying on the floor with her head in the shower recess. Her hair and face were wet and her top was around her neck, exposing pale skin, almost-breasts. The psycho-tweenies dispersed, smirking, and their victim hastily covered up.

I bore down on them like a Mama Lion. 'What's going on?'

Little helium voices squeaked, 'Nothing.' They pushed past me and skittered outside. I helped the girl to her feet. She was skinny and awkward and her skin was so pale it had a blue tinge.

'Are you okay? Did they hurt you?'

The girl didn't answer. She straightened her clothes and walked over to the sink. I followed her and watched as she bent her head and started wringing out her hair. She tied it back with an elastic band and smiled at me in the mirror. 'They wanted to see my witch's tit.'

'Your what?'

'I have three nipples. Only the third one is just like a birthmark. Janey and that say it's the mark of the devil.'

'What?' It took me a few seconds to absorb this. Then: 'Bullies,' I said tersely.

The girl said, 'They do it every year. It's like a tradition.'

We walked out together. My Spirit Ranch map ended at the toilet block, but I could see a path beyond it that went Further.

'What's down there?' I asked the girl.

'The recycling cage. Fraser's house. He used to be the owner but he died. He went into the desert and never came back out. He was wearing his underpants and he had face paint on. Bird says he was a visionary.'

'Who's Bird?'

'My brother.'

'Is he here?' I asked. 'Why doesn't he look after you?'

'He has special duties. We both do. Bird looks after the wildlife and I look after the . . . domestic side of things. It's how we pay our way.'

The girl stared across the plains, wrinkling her nose at a group of kids kicking a soccer ball around. Then she turned back and without warning gave me swift hug. 'I'm Olive,' she said in my ear. 'Hug back. Janey and that, they're looking.'

I hugged back. It felt weird but not awful. She smelled like a mixed bag of lollies: milk bottles and musk sticks.

I stepped back and straightened my sleeves. Olive said, 'I think they'll leave me alone now. Thanks.' She ran off, with her face all aglow, like she was carrying a present and she knew what it was, and it was good. I turned and faced the wild. Somewhere out there was the desert, then Nhill, then the world. I couldn't remember the last time I'd been hugged so hard.

POETIC AND CONDEMNED

Fraser's house rose out of the scrub like a sandstone dream. It had a tin roof, jasmine fringing, detached gutters and nasturtiums crowding the cracks in the porch. I peered in a window and saw ghosted furniture and books and newspapers in ceiling-high stacks. The front door was locked, but the door to the adjoining garage was swinging open. I nudged it and wandered in.

I like traditional men's spaces – sheds, garages, urinals (joke). In our old house Dad stored his 'little village' in the roof. His little village started as a train set and just kept growing. Mum used to call it his girlfriend. She was only half joking. Dad, who could be waffly about so many things, was never anything but driven in there. I would sneak in sometimes. I wouldn't touch anything. I just liked the way the room felt. It had an air of purpose. I could tell he dreamt stuff up in there. Fraser's garage had the same feel.

Through a maze of jerry cans and jam jars stood a tarp-covered monolith. The sun made crazy patterns on it and I traced them with my finger. I tugged at a corner. Underneath was an old VW – a lovebug, or some kind of lovebug mutation. I looked down and saw that it was on blocks. There were other bits and pieces of the car family scattered about, giving the place a wrecker's allure, but I knew about places like this – they're all about possibility and potential, nothing actually *works*.

The back garden was only just contained by its crumbling stone wall. It looked poetic and condemned – in other words, perfect. There was a rockery with spilling-over wildflowers, and over a little hill there was even an old roundabout. I wandered around the space dreamily, plucking and breathing in lavender. Eventually I arranged myself on the roundabout and dug in my bag for my cigarettes.

I started smoking when I met Chloe. This was reason number one for Dad to hate her. All the breath mints in the world couldn't disguise the fact that every night I stuck my head out of my bedroom window and puffed away like a caboose. But this was where dreaming began. Smoking was like a physical ellipsis. I drew back and my mind went dot . . . dot . . . dot . . . For the length of the cigarette I could be anyone. In my dreams I was usually thin and untouchable. Boys would swarm. Occasionally I would talk to one, or let one carry my schoolbag, or set fire to himself in the street outside my house.

Chloe's best bag-lady joke was that she only smoked after sex – and she was down to two packs a day. I lit up and toasted my absent friend. Then I wrenched the wheel and lay down and let the swirling trees and sky and sunspots hypnotise me into something like happiness.

Thursday night, Ben Sebatini's: I walk through the door in a gold dress, with glitter on my eyelids, cheeks and lips. Ben Seb sees me and does a triple take. He says, 'I can't believe you're really here.'

I laugh throatily. 'Believe it, baby.'

'Come on.' He grabs my hand and starts leading me through the throng. 'I want to be alone with you.'

I laugh incredulously, 'You're going to leave your own party?'

He looks back at the fray. 'Those people are bores . . . but you, Riley, you –'

And I stop under the streetlight and say, 'What?'

He shakes his head. 'You know.'

'Tell me,' I whisper.

He holds my hand and swings it in a slow circle. He pulls me towards him. 'There's no one else like you,' he says. And then he kisses me and it's like every cell in my body is atomised.

I was still in dreamland when the roundabout jerked to a stop. I looked up to see a boy holding onto the rail, one foot up on the platform and the other on the ground. His stance was at odds with his gawkward appearance: pipe cleaner legs, ramekin ears. He was wearing an outdoorsy canvas vest with a hundred compartments. A pair of binoculars hung from his neck.

'You're not supposed to be here,' he said. 'You're Out of Bounds.'

'Ok-ay,' I eyed him warily. 'Are you a counsellor?'

'No.'

'So that means you're Out of Bounds too?'

'No. I have work to do here.' He looked down hastily. He was trying to suppress a smile, but he was losing the battle. He really had to concentrate to make his mouth do what he wanted it to. He shook his head once, twice, three times, fit-ishly. Then he pointed with his arm at a right angle to his body. 'You have to go. '

'Okay, I'm going.' I ground my cigarette into the sand, and stared at him trying to work him out. He was Not Quite Right. An NQR bird nerd boy. Chloe would love it. He lifted his head and something in his expression – both eagerness *and* hesitance – reminded me of Olive. 'Wait,' I said. 'Are you Bird?'

He looked shocked. 'Who told you?'

I laughed. 'A little bird.'

'What kind?'

I started to laugh again, but Bird was dead serious.

'Um . . . a magpie?' I improvised.

He opened his mouth and spoke in the polished voice of a television presenter. 'Australian Magpie. Member of the Artamidae family. Diurnal. Omnivorous. Mostly a ground-feeder but will eat human food. May eat its own digestive products. This piebald bird is used to both bush and urban surroundings. Beware the magpie during nesting season (aka swooping season) and lock up your jewellery, for the magpie is attracted to bright and shiny things and has no qualms about stealing whatever takes its fancy.'

Bird stopped reciting. I remembered a story I'd once read about a woman who finds a transistor in her false tooth. When she opened her mouth the radio would come out –

race-calls, talkback, classic hits.

'What did you have for breakfast?' I asked him. 'An ornithologist?'

Bird cocked his head. He moved in and I had nowhere to go but back. I don't know what I *thought* he was going to do – push me? Kiss me? And I don't know why I thought these things first. In the end all he did was touch the skin above my chest. 'You should put some sunscreen on.' He smiled and suddenly looked about ten years old. He shouted, 'This is my place!' and kicked the roundabout, hard. The wheel spun and my cigs and lavender sprigs went sliding out onto the soft dirt.

'Thank you, Psycho!' I bent down to collect my things. But he was already gone, storming up the stairs and into the garage. The screen door shuddered in his wake.

ORIENTATION

Just metres away from me, on a small stage, Counsellor Roslyn of the nightmare hair and mushroom-coloured jumpsuit was leading the group in a song. The song seemed to only have two lines and the younger campers sang it with gusto: *Let JESUS in. Let his Spir-it SHINE!* The older campers – and I could only spot a handful – were more self-conscious. A boy sitting near me with bad acne and wanker's jangle was moving his lips but no sound came out. I looked at his nametag. Richard. Next to him the speccy bubbler boy was nodding along. His nametag was also clearly displayed. Ethan. The song went forever. Roslyn was dancing but her brain must have been sending mixed messages; her pelvis didn't know where to look. If I'd had my phone I'd have snapped her for Chloe.

Out of the forty-odd campers the majority were under twelve and over-enthusiastic to the point of psychosis. When they sang 'Jesus' they closed their eyes and waved their hands in the air. In and around that there was smiling. Lots of smiling. These kids were shiny-clean and cling-wrapped.

They made me feel like a big, dirty *outlaw* and while part of me felt proud of my difference, another part just felt . . . bleak. Lonely. I sat back, hugging my knees, and let the veil of blah fall over me. *Three days*, I reminded myself, *Three days, not seven, and then a big, beautiful Ben Sebatini reward.*

Now that the tape-recorded music had faded, Roslyn produced a brass bugle. She hunched her shoulders and blew and the noise was like pure pain. After she stopped my ears were still ringing. Roslyn took a humble bow. 'Thank you, thank you! That's the breakfast bugle. When you hear that you know tucker's up!' Roslyn had a monotone. Her words all ran together like wet ink. When she stopped to take a breath she almost lost her balance. She teetered on the spot, and everybody waited.

'Campers, on your nametags you'll find a feather. That feather represents your group. Hands up who has a white feather?'

Many hands shot up.

'Ter-rif-ic. If you have a white feather that mean you're in the Mallee group. Who has a brown feather?'

Slightly less hands showed.

'Okay, brown feathers are Bronzewings. If you have a yellow feather you're a Honeyeater, okay? Ter-rif-ic. Okay, people, go find your people!'

I dug around my bag for my nametag. I was a yellow feather. Honeyeater. Sarita flashed her nametag at me. She was also a yellow feather. I put my palm up. *How*. She came over and sat too close and the other Honeyeaters followed. There was eight of us: Sarita, Fleur, Richard, Ethan, the curious Bird, two girl twins with identical nun-cuts and myself. Ter-rif-ic.

Counsellor Neville patrolled the stage with a cordless microphone and told an interminable story about how driving down he got a flat tyre which led to an epiphany about just how small he was, but just how perfectly he fitted into the physical world . . . 'The clouds were rolling across the sky. The trees seemed to be breathing – I felt so ALIVE. I remembered to thank God. It seems so obvious, but how often do we take time out – to sit and think and appreciate – but most of all to thank God? I took Time Out. I sat on the bonnet of my Volvo and watched the colours spread in the sky, until the sun had sunk completely.' Neville tucked the microphone under his arm and clasped his hands together. 'Let's thank Him now.'

Heads bowed around me. I picked at my cuticles.

For me the whole God thing was imposs. Godliness was next to dubiousness. If the Christian kids at my high school were anything to go by, then camp was going to be a big smile full of bad teeth. Those kids were creepy. They talked Alpha and Hillsong like it was a new slang and they wouldn't budge in their beliefs if you hit them over the head with a dinosaur bone. Before the Norma Trauma I'd been to church maybe three times in my life. Dad used to be a 'lapsed' Catholic. Now he as good as says that Mum was the lapse-factor.

I wondered if she was watching. If she could see me now she'd be laughing, rolling her eyes, going 'Jay-sus!' Like she used to say to Dad when she wanted to piss him off. Mum was fat like me. She was dotty and over-dramatic. When she found out about the cancer she howled like a howler monkey. I remember her stomping around the backyard. 'I will not go gracefully, I will not.' But as she got weaker her anger faded.

First comes acceptance, then transcendence.

In the early months, none of us brought up the D that follows the C, but one day I asked Mum what she thought would happen and she said, 'I'm picturing sunshine, straight up. Someone will take my hand and I'll feel light. When I was pregnant with you I used to float in a saltwater pool. I've decided it will be light as that. Just *Light*.'

At the funeral everyone talked about God and Heaven and how Mum wasn't in pain anymore, but the priest kept calling her 'Lily' – no one *ever* called Mum Lily! – and the funeral had hidden costs, and the whole thing just felt heavy, not light at all.

THE IDEA OF KINSHIP

Towards the end of Neville's holy thanks the door opened. A guy ran down the side of the room, pumping his fist like a game-show contestant. He did a heroic leap onto the stage and took the chair next to Roslyn. He was *gorgeous*. He had white-blond hair in a kind of faux-hawk, brown eyes and olive skin. I stared at him from under my hat. He looked too young to be a counsellor. Over the top of the T-shirt he had a black-and-silver vest with the letters YL. Neville introduced him as Craig Barrett, Youth Leader. *There's a challenge*, I told myself, echoing my father. My first instinct was to put him in the too-hard basket. *A guy like that and a girl like me . . .* but then he smiled and, ohmystars! It was the kind of smile a guy gives you when he's just about to pull your school uniform over your head and expose your bra to all and sundry. The kind of smile that killed me.

In my dreamy-dreams I'd imagine a boy, sarcastic and hilarious, who'd make me a fetish necklace out of gumnuts and feathers and champagne wire. A boy like that could be possible. But a beautiful boy was something else. A beautiful boy could make me feel beautiful back.

Craig was squinting at the door, waving someone in. At first all I saw was a dark square in the sunlight. It came closer. I realised it was a guy in a wheelchair. Craig pointed him to Honeyeater territory. He parked across from me and bowed his head. I checked him out: he was skinny and pale. He had long dark hair and a cool bruiser's pout. He was wearing a Kreator T-shirt and black jeans but I could tell by the way his feet fell that the chair was a fixture. His eyes flashed sideways. *Busted.* I stared down at my lapful of lavender. I lined the flowers up head to head.

When Craig took the stage an appreciative ripple went through the audience. The female campers sat up straighter, even little Mallee girls who still played with Barbies. But Craig did have a bit of Ken Doll about him. Fleur did a languid neck roll so that her hair fell over one shoulder. Craig looked comfortable with all this attention. He read the rules, with one eyebrow cocked for coolness.

'No drinking, no drugs, no pranks – you know what I'm talking about – no short-sheeting, no Glad Wrap over the toilet seat. Take it from me – if you stick your roomie's hand in a bowl of warm water while he's sleeping he will *not* wet the bed. Ahem. No stealing, no phones, no unauthorised excursions into non-camp territory, no midnight feasts . . . Did I mention no swearing? No inappropriate clothing, no coupling up . . .' He mimed 'NOT'.

There were giggles at that. Sarita's eyes were all pupil. She looked like she'd stopped breathing. Craig's words kept coming. They folded over each other like lather. The Mallees were getting restless. There was sneaker scraping going on. Beyond the rec room walls I could hear nature noises: birds and insects, summer's fizz. I could feel someone looking at me – Wheelchair Boy. I smiled at him. He rolled his eyes and I tingled all over at the idea of kinship.

'One more thing,' Craig called. 'Roslyn has lost her "shroud" – so keep your eyes peeled for a – '

Roslyn lunged at the microphone, ' – piece of fabric. If you find it, *please* don't wash it . . . or use it as a hanky. Just . . . hand it in. Ter-rif-ic.' She smiled at us all for a few seconds too long and then sat back down.

Just when I thought it was all over, there was Neville again.

He said, 'We have some old friends and some new faces. If you treat the new faces like old friends then it's going to be a beautiful time for everyone.' He raised his head. 'Dylan Luck, would you come up please?'

Wheelchair Boy came forward slowly until his tyres bumped the foot of the stage. For a second no one did anything then Craig and Neville lifted the chair onto the stage. Neville said, 'Some of you know Dylan from previous camps. You may not have seen him since his accident. He's still Dylan and he'd appreciate your support and friendship. Don't be strangers!'

Dylan stared above our heads to the back of the room. He didn't look embarrassed. He didn't look anything. Some of the younger kids were staring, with dropped jaws. 'Accident' is such a non-word, so non-specific. Neville made it sound like nothing, but here was this boy in a wheelchair, and you couldn't call a wheelchair 'nothing'. I recalled Fleur and Sarita's mystery boy who'd jumped sixteen floors – and realised he and Dylan had to be one and the same.

Neville went on. 'Dylan, we've got something for you – because we value you, and because you deserve it.'

Craig came forward. 'Here you go, dude.' He clamped a hand on Dylan's shoulder and handed him a shiny bundle. Dylan was slow to unfold it, too slow for Craig, who moved across and shook it out and held it up for display. It was a vest identical to his. Craig draped it over Dylan's shoulders and announced: 'So this year there's two Youth Leaders!' He turned to show his letters and everyone clapped. I clapped too – I was bored. I was getting delirious again. I whistled and threw my lavender sprigs at the stage. A flower landed on Dylan's chest. He watched it fall to his lap and then he picked it up. I noticed his cross then: thick and silver, hanging on a thin leather string. As he held the sprig of lavender, his face changed and I had a sudden flash that he looked on the outside how I felt on the inside: Lost. Moody. Superior. Charged.

Dylan smelled the flower and stared straight at me. Then he put it in his mouth and ate it.

REFERENCE WORK

Orientation was over but you wouldn't know it for the amount of hang-back. It was a whole new hubbub of hugs and memories. I took the opportunity to hunt down a phone. The counsellors' annexe was too close for comfort. I walked back around the main building until I was standing outside Neville's office. His door was locked from the inside but the louvred windows were open wide enough for me to snake my arm in. I felt around for the doorknob, mentally preparing my defence. *Your honour*, I'd say, *you can't call it breaking and entering when it's this easy.* I went straight for the phone. Chloe picked up on the third ring.

'My friend, my friend!' she greeted me. 'Are you there yet?'
'I am.'
'And?'
'Hell.'
'Expand.'
'There's nothing here. It's a desert. I feel like an Arab.'
'Let me see what I can do.'
We laughed our bawdy-house laughs.

'BTW thanks for the book.'

'I told you I'd get you out of it.' I could hear Chloe smiling. She took a special pleasure in sorting me out. This would become one of her stories.

'Now all I've got to do is make it to Wednesday.'

'My advice is treat it like a prison term. Embark on a course of self-improvement. Do crunches, learn sign language. Don't wash your hair. If you let the grease build up it actually makes it stronger *and* shinier.'

'Thank you John Frieda.'

She tried to make me smile. 'Is there no hotness? No cute, virginal Jesus-boys? All trembling and stuttering and eager to please?'

'No, they're more your acnefarious kid-brother types.'

We laughed again. I felt a little bit better. But Chloe was still laughing, and I had a sudden picture of her holding the phone a small distance from her mouth, flicking the edges of her Hello Kitty decals. Chloe started dishing about some guy and my eyes roved to the camp photos on Neville's walls. In one frame there were two pictures. The first was the human pyramid photo from the camp program. The second was of the campers clowning around pre-assembly. I spotted Craig, standing back to back with a hot guy. They were clearly the comedy duo, arms folded, smart-arse smiles. I stepped in closer, and almost gasped. Craig's hot friend was Dylan, the Wheelchair Boy. He had the same silver cross but other than that he could have been a different person. His hair was short. His body was fit. He was tanned and his face was non-puffy. He looked directly at the camera with an expression that was rambunctious and joyous and self-satisfied all at once. He had presence, but more than that, he had Stature.

'Are you listening to me?' Chloe asked.

'I'd better go.'

'My friend, my friend . . .'

I hung up, feeling weird. Chloe seemed a long way away.

Chloe's moniker for me came from an Anne Sexton poem that Sky, our patchouli lit teacher, was obsessed with. Chloe could never remember the next line but I knew it by heart: *My friend, my friend, I was born doing reference work in sin and born confessing it.* The poem was about a cross Anne Sexton's friend had given her to wear – and she'd worn it, but it hadn't helped. I could see Sky now, leaning on her desk, lowering her silver reading glasses to show us her moist eyes, as she repeated the kicker. '*Need is not quite belief.*'

Anne Sexton had been through some things and committed suicide. I guessed Dylan had been through some things too – but he was still here and still wearing his cross. I wondered if he'd ever taken it off.

Bad-Weird and Jesus-Freaky

The mess hall was alive with noise and clatter. The tables were set out in ascending rows from Mallee to Bronzewing to Honeyeater. The counsellors' table was on a small platform under a mural of The Last Supper. It was so obviously painted by kids: the disciples had bung eyes and wonky smiles and for some reason, Jesus had a ponytail.

I headed straight for the servery. Dinner was lasagne, dry as a nun's knickers and probably just as tasty. While I struggled to identify the vegetarian option, I could feel eyes on me. It was Olive, the girl I'd saved from the psycho-tweenies. She stood behind the servery in an apron, beaming. *Special domestic duties*, I thought. *Huh.*

Olive said, 'Take the lasagne. Trust me. You don't want the lentil casserole.'

I held my tray out and watched her put a super-sized serving onto it. She followed it up with a big slice of cheesecake. She leaned in. 'Anything you need, come see me.' I looked down at my loaded tray. It couldn't hurt to have a friend in the kitchen.

At the Honeyeaters' table I tried to ignore the tragic palette of older teens. The order went: Richard, Ethan and the twins (Lisa and Laura, or Laura and Lisa, they were indistinguishable) on one side, Fleur, Bird, Sarita and myself on the other. There were empty chairs at the head and foot, presumably for Craig and Dylan. Last I'd seen of Dylan he was parked on the rec room stage watching the centipede of legs rush for the mess hall. I didn't know where Craig was. I had *Utopia* open on the table in front of me like a shield. I ate quickly and eavesdropped on the insane ramblings of zealots.

'What's a shroud?' Ethan wanted to know.

Richard spoke with authority. 'You know, like the Shroud of Turin.'

'Huh?'

'A *miracle*.' Richard was clearly a Man of Knowledge. 'Did you hear about that toasted cheese sandwich that looked like the Virgin Mary that sold on eBay for thousands of dollars?'

'What?'

'Believe it.' Richard said. 'The lady who sold it said it never went mouldy and it gave her good luck. She had it for years.'

Ethan asked, 'Do you think it works, Roslyn's shroud? What do you think she does with it?'

'Late at night, she lies on the sofa and presses it against her face.'

Ethan said, 'She probably just keeps it to ward off Satan. That's what I'd do. She must be really panicking without it.'

'She'll just have to pray harder,' Richard concluded.

I could feel Sarita's eyes boring through the cloth boards. I lowered my tome. 'Do you *have* to watch me eat?'

'Sorry.' She smiled and pushed her plate across. 'Do you want this?'

I considered the slice of cloudy cheesecake. 'Okay.' I ate a forkful of the sugary mess. Then another, and another. I ate without tasting. At one point I looked up and saw that Richard and Ethan were both staring at me like I was an outrage.

Richard smirked. 'Comfort eating?'

Ethan snickered. I decided I hated them. They were like Roslyn's children – bad-weird and Jesus-freaky. Sarita put her hand on mine, and pressed it lightly, then took it away. 'How is it that you came to be here?' she asked, in her funny, lilting voice.

'I got sent down for bad behaviour.'

Sarita waited.

'My dad's girlfriend, Norma,' I told her. 'She's on her stepmother L-plates. She thinks she knows what's good for me.'

'They don't often take new people. Most of us have been coming here since we were Mallees.' Sarita paused. 'What kind of bad behaviour?'

I waved my fork around. 'You know, sex, drugs, rock'n'roll.'

She let out a nervous laugh. I looked at her, 'You do know?'

'Of course!' Her face had gone beet-red.

'Sure you do,' I muttered, letting my fork clang down. 'Look at you. You're so fresh, you've still got the tag on.'

Sarita flinched, and I felt a little mean.

'So you know everyone here, then?' I asked.

Sarita nodded. She looked across at the twins. 'They're new.'

We both watched Craig lope past. He sat down with the counsellors.

'What's his story?' I asked Sarita. 'He's a Honeyeater, isn't he? Why isn't he sitting with us?'

Sarita looked cagey. 'Youth Leader privilege.' She lowered her voice. 'He gets his own cabin too.'

I raised my eyebrows. 'Interesting. Tell me more.'

Sarita opened her mouth. It was like someone had taken the cork out. She didn't talk about Craig specifically, she talked camp – the positives (good to be away from family life, great to have like-minded people to play-and-pray with); the negatives (some people – and she didn't want to name names – thought they were a bit good); and a whole lot of guff in the middle (best games, worst dinners). Regarding the counsellors, Neville was a known softie – 'He believes in hug therapy.' She pointed to the meathead counsellor. 'But Anton – he believes in punishing the body with extreme sports.'

'So they're like Good Cop/Bad Cop,' I said. 'What about Roslyn?'

Sarita smiled. 'Roslyn has the Holy Spirit running through her like a river.'

'Ah, yes. I was admiring her jumpsuit earlier.'

Sarita looked blank. Sarcasm was lost on her.

'Why are there so few Honeyeaters?'

Sarita shrugged.

'You think it's something to do with the fact that most sixteen-year-olds are out in the world, fulfilling the requirements of their legal age?'

'I don't understand.'

'I'll draw you a picture.'

Sarita's eyes went wide and she blushed again and gave me a sissy slap. I laughed. I wasn't used to shocking people. Chloe was shockproof.

I watched Craig cruise the desserts. He arrived at our table, squeezed into the seat near Fleur and attempted to spoon-feed her his cheesecake. She shook her head and patted her non-existent stomach. 'Give it to the new girl.'

Craig's smile was leery. 'You're Riley, right? Weird name.'

'Not really. My mother wanted me to have fun, the life of Riley . . . '

'And are you . . . having fun?'

His voice dropped. Our eyes locked. I felt like a contract was being drawn up – a silent contract that said something was going to happen between us. A hush seemed to fall over the Honeyeaters' table. Sarita looked from Craig to me to Fleur. Fleur had been cutting her pineapple ring with a knife and fork. She looked at me with gunfight eyes. I pictured her spitting a slug into the spittoon, '*Hombre – are you ready to DIE? I'm gonna string you up like a Chinatown chicken.*'

In real life she leaned into Craig. 'I learnt those songs you sent me. When are we going to practise?' She fluffed his hair. His eyes stayed on me. I slammed my book shut and got ready to leave. Fleur was thin and pretty, but she had ice queen written all over her. Chloe says access beats beauty every time.

'Where are you going?' Craig wanted to know.

'Who cares?' Fleur said.

'She's going to have a cigarette,' Sarita whispered.

As I walked away I tried to picture what they saw: my crazy curves, my straw bag swinging, my hat in my hand sweeping the air. I bet they'd never seen a big girl so confident. Boom-boom-BOOM. My mules clacked on the cork floor like castanets. *Arriba!*

LUCKY SMOKE

I walked across the plain looking for a place to smoke. There was Fraser's house but I'd eaten too much to walk that far, and I didn't want to run into Bird, whose special duties no doubt included narking on wayward campers. Then, just past the toilets I found the spot – a bench behind an old incinerator. The site afforded a clear view of the plain, but was far away enough to hide the evidence should the enemy approach. I sat down and lit up. I had a few seconds of grand defiance, but then that good feeling started to slide. Even though I was hidden, I felt conspicuous. What was I doing? Sucking smoke into my lungs and blowing it back out again? The heat had died down a little. The sky had gone orange.

Dylan came windmilling down the gravel path. He was fast. He looked deranged. He parked next to me and pulled a smoke from behind his ear. He was wearing fingerless leather biker gloves. They were so anti they made me smile.

'Match me,' he said.

'What?'

'Match me; light my fire.'

'Oh, okay.' I lit his cigarette. He didn't thank me; he simply puffed away and stared at the streaky sky. The campers started to pile out of the mess hall. They bolted and skipped and chased and dawdled across the plain. Dylan and I sat side-by-side. As soon as I stubbed my cigarette out, Dylan offered me his pack. I noticed that he had a lucky smoke turned upside down. I liked that. I didn't suppose the Wheelchair Boy would be much on luck, but there it was, third from the end. I took the one next to it. Then I remembered that his surname was Luck. I wondered how he felt about that. I was wondering about his 'accident' too. I almost asked: *What happened to you?* But something stopped me. He probably had to answer *that* question all the time. I wouldn't ask it. I'd never ask it. If he jumped sixteen floors he must have had a good reason.

I studied him again – and this time I didn't care that he knew. If I could stare him into conversation, well, that had to be better than all this sit-and-no-talk business. His chair looked banged up. It had a series of scratches along the side, like days marked off in fishbone lines of five, hundreds of them. And then there were the DIY Playboy mudflaps – *so* trucker fucker. I decided that Dylan was an ally with a highly developed sense of irony. The YL vest over his Kreator T-shirt made a nice contradiction. His bag was graffed up with band names I didn't recognise – lightning bolts and heavy metal *umlauts*.

'Are you a metal-head?' I asked him.

Nothing. Dylan's muteness was starting to make me feel irrelevant, so I went all out, interviewing him. I threw random questions in the air and watched them disappear with the cigarette smoke.

'What really happens when you play Led Zeppelin backwards?'

'What's your porn star name?'

'Do you have any piercings?'

'What do you like in a girl?'

'Beavis or Butthead?'

'Elvis or Marilyn?'

'Jesus or George Bush?'

'Where's the weirdest place you ever had sex?'

'How many Christians does it take to change a lightbulb?'

Then I noticed the white cord running down to his bag. He had earplugs in. *Oh.*

'Hey!' I yanked the cord out of his ear. 'I was talking to you.'

He put his earplugs away, and looked down at his feet. Maybe he was shy. Definitely he was weird. Either way he still wasn't talking. I watched him dig in his pocket and take out a vial. He shook out two white pills, put one on his tongue and swallowed.

I was so used to his brick wall pose that when he finally looked at me *I* went mute. Dylan's eyes were heavy-lidded, grave and grey. He silently offered me the other pill.

'What'll it do?'

Dylan raised his eyebrows, daring me.

'Okay,' I said, taking the pill.

Craig bounded up to us then, his lips quirked into a half-smile. 'Bonding over carcinogenics? Why am I not surprised?'

He worked his Youth Leader schtick. 'Just make sure you extinguish the butts. This is tinderbox country.'

Dylan made a noise that was somewhere between a scoff and a snort.

Craig repositioned himself so that he was standing in front of us with his arms folded. 'We're setting up for night cricket.' He nodded to Dylan. 'Wanna umpire?'

Nothing.

'What about you?' Craig was looking at me like he knew all my secrets.

'No thanks.'

Craig looked momentarily put out. Then he palmed his faux-hawk, issued a 'Laters' and strode over to where some Mallees were teasing a frog with a torch.

Dylan and I watched him go. We turned to each other.

'*Laters.*'

We said it at the same time with the same wince, then we smiled and looked away. I watched Craig parade across the plain, gathering players. He was showing a lot of leg in his tighty-whitey shorts. Maybe I was gazing, because Dylan spoke up and when he did his voice was a shock to the silence. He said, 'If you want to get on *that*, ask him about the time he saved Sarita's life.'

'What makes you think I want to "get on that"?'

'All girls go for Craig. Your whole frothy gothy flower-wielding shit doesn't fool me.'

I looked at him. I couldn't tell if he was being serious or not. And now it seemed as though I was mistaken in recognising the kinship between us. I wanted to talk to him more, but he started twitching in his chair, lifting and lowering his butt, patting and prodding his legs. I decided he was trying to unnerve me. And I decided that I wouldn't let him.

Fleur was walking towards the toilet. Dylan suddenly shoved his hands down on his wheels and shouted, 'Fleur – wait up!' She must have heard him but she just about-faced and walked faster, away from him. Dylan went off-road. It was a tragi-comic sight to see this sad-eyed wheelchair boy getting bogged in the woodchip, but by then the pill he'd given me had started to take. My eyelids were drooping like sails. I staggered back to the cabin and fell in a heap on the bed.

Sarita was wearing the full cricket whites. Clearly borrowed. She was swimming in them. 'Aren't you playing?' she asked.

I didn't even have the energy to laugh. I closed my eyes. One day down, two to go. Could I do it? Maybe if I stayed like this – drugged up, *in absentia*. As I drifted off to the sound of night cricket and real crickets I styled the *Vanity Fair* Spirit Ranch photo-spread in my mind. Craig and Fleur were the Ken and Barbie, Sarita was the Quiet One, Bird was the Wild Card, the twins were the Empty Vessels Waiting To Be Filled, Richard was the Professor. Ethan was the Collaborator. I was the Drama, and Dylan –

Dylan was the Darkness.

ON THE SECOND DAY

DRAMA QUEENS

I woke up to the sound of the PA squealing. There was a loud *clunk* and then Roslyn's voice came through, bigger than life.

'Attention campers. This is your thought for the morning: *Lord, let me live adventurously today, flinging my whole self into all I do.*'

The PA squealed and clunked again, and she was gone. I sat up, feeling confused. Sarita was perched on the end of my bed, smiling at me.

'Oh God.' I blinked. 'Where am I? What's going on?'

'You missed a good one,' she said. 'Night cricket went until nine and then we had campfire singing. Craig played guitar – he's really good – and Fleur sang harmony. She sings through her nose.'

She looked down, her mouth turned inward.

'They went off somewhere. And look – her bed hasn't been slept in.'

I ignored the lick of jealousy and rolled my eyes. 'So much for "no coupling up". Are they boyfriend-girlfriend then?'

'I think so,' Sarita said. 'But it's bad.'

'What do you mean – because of Jesus?' I joked.

Sarita nodded. 'That. And also because last summer Fleur and Dylan were . . .' She laced her hands together and pressed hard. 'And then he had the . . . accident . . . She hasn't even talked to him yet. He looks so different.'

'Different how?' I asked even though I knew.

'He used to be athletic and competitive. He and Craig were like the two sides of the same coin.'

'You mean they were nothing like each other?'

'No, I mean they were exactly like each other.'

'That would be a double-headed coin then.'

One corner of Sarita's mouth tilted up. 'Yes.'

I thought about Dylan flying after Fleur. About Craig's sulk when Dylan refused to umpire. 'What happened to him?'

'I heard it was a suicide attempt. Richard said it was a surfing accident.'

'Has anyone actually asked Dylan how it happened?'

Sarita bit her lip and shook her head.

I asked, 'You know him, don't you?'

'Yes but . . .' Sarita started. 'He's broken. I overheard Neville talking to Roslyn about him. He said he'd asked Dylan if he wanted a carer, but Dylan said no, he could look after himself.'

'God,' I said, almost to myself. 'How would you be?'

'Fleur doesn't deserve him,' Sarita said.

'Dylan?'

'No! Craig.'

I opened my mouth to tell her what I thought of Craig, how he fell into the HBNQR category (hot-but-not-quite-right) but the demented glint in her eye made me save it. Sarita was a believer. She had the woolly balaclava of bullshit stretched over her eyes. She'd see heavenly hosts of angels before she saw Craig's trail of sleaze. Not that I was immune. I hadn't forgotten that look the Youth Leader had given me. He'd cameo-ed in my dreams and I'd already decided that if he wanted to, I would. Might as well have something to brag to Chloe about.

Sarita had her head in her hands and was staring dreamily at nothing.

'Are you having lustful thoughts?' I teased her.

I thought she'd laugh with me, but she hung her head and cringed. '*Please* don't tell anyone.' Then she pressed her palms into the bedspread and whispered, 'I wish I was *dead*!'

I crawled down the bed. I knelt in front of Sarita, cleared her hair away from her face and pressed my thumbs to her temples. This was something Mum used to do to me whenever I went over the top. 'Here.'

'What are you doing?' Sarita sniffed.

'I'm handing over my Drama Queen crown. Take it, it's yours.'

Sarita looked at me warily. I almost ducked. Just in case that was too much, just in case she was going to Crack. But no. She took a breath. She drew herself up to a queenly pose and gave a little wave to I, the commoner. Then she giggled uncontrollably for a full minute.

'Steady,' I said, smiling. 'It's not *that* funny.'

Sarita sobered up, 'I am glad you're here.' She nodded and looked towards the door. 'And now I'm going to perform my ablutions.'

'I don't need to know that.'

Sarita picked up her wash-bag and towel. As she walked out, I saw something flutter down to the floor. I called after her, 'You dropped something.' Sarita either didn't hear me or didn't care. The screen door bounced against its frame. I stretched over the bed and reached across the floor until my fingers found the lost property, a square of mould-mottled cotton that had once been white. Holy eBay miracle! It was Roslyn's missing shroud. I held it up to the window and the face of Jesus came through the murk. If I scrunched it a certain way it looked like he was winking. I lay back on the bed and pressed the shroud to my face. It smelt like aniseed.

CAPSIZED!

In full flight Dylan's voice had a wry, larrikin backhand.

'Craig's got a tight walk,' he observed. 'More like a strut. It's like his dick is the centre of his existence. You can tell a lot about a person by the way they walk.'

'What does mine say?'

'You walk like you think people are watching.' He paused. 'Only I don't think anyone is.'

'You're probably right.' I sighed.

We were sitting on the landing while the other Honeyeaters and Counsellor Anton hauled canoes from the dock into the river. In Spirit Ranch speak this was our first 'off-site activity'. We'd come down on the mini-bus. Dylan got on last. He had two crutches attached to the back of his wheelchair. With the exception of Craig, who was acting as man on the ground, the Honeyeaters acted like seeing Dylan ditch his chair was completely uninteresting. They talked amongst themselves or looked out the opposite window. But they didn't fool me. I could tell each and every one was sneaking a look when they thought they could get away with it. I decided to be blatant. I pressed my face against the window, made a blowfish and kept watching.

Dylan's manoeuvre from chair to crutches was slicker than I thought it would be. Craig rushed to help him fold his wheelchair but it was like watching someone trying to fathom IKEA assemblage. Dylan watched him with a perverse smile on his face before pointing out a release button. He came towards the mini-bus, frowning as he pressed down on his crutches, dragging his feet in the dirt. The twins were sitting in front of me. I heard one of them say something about a marionette. I punched the back of the seat and when they turned around looking all wounded, I did it again, harder.

Bird was looking through his binoculars. He pointed to something and jumped with excitement. 'Anton! Anton!'

'This had better be good.' Anton snatched Bird's binoculars and squinted into them. He handed them back without a word. Bird slumped. Richard threw a date at him. Craig stowed Dylan's chair and we were away. I was not a nature girl – but it felt great to leave the compound. As the shadow of the arches fell across my seat I waved my hands. '*Hallelujah!*'

When we arrived at the river I had the sense of other creatures scarpering. The world seemed eerily still, broken only by the occasional snap-buzz of a dragonfly. The river was wide and brown and slow. There was no natural bank on the opposite side, just blackberry bush and ancient river gums. They were huge, intimidating. They punched the sky, and the clouds hung around them like groupies.

'Get into pairs!' Anton barked. I avoided Sarita's eye and moved backwards until I was next to Dylan, who was back in his chair. He looked at me like I was mad.

'I don't do sports,' I found myself confessing.

'Why not?' He looked at me suspiciously.

I thought of PE teachers-slash-sadists, of trying to stand proud when no one wanted me on their team, of thigh-rub rash and straitjacket skin and my only options being heart attack or hurl.

'I don't like to sweat,' I said simply.

'That's a shame,' Dylan said. 'I like sweaty girls.'

'Okay everybody!' Anton roared. 'Lifejackets *on*! Helmets *on*!'

Dylan and I stared at the pairs: Lisa and Laura, Richard and Ethan, Bird and Sarita. Fleur sat in her canoe waiting for Craig but he was heading over our way . . . again.

'Here we go,' Dylan said under his breath.

Craig squatted down next to Dylan. 'You could have a go. If you want. I'll be your partner. Or Anton could.'

Dylan shook his head.

'Okay . . .' Craig backed off. He went back to the bank, frowning, and said something to Anton.

'Fuck it,' Dylan got his cigarettes out and lit one. 'Youth Leaders should only exist out of frame.'

'Wait. I thought you were a Youth Leader.'

'Yeah, well.' He frowned down at his vest. Then he passed me a cassette tape. 'Check this out. Neville made it for me.'

Sure enough, 'Neville Special' was scrawled across the spine.

Dylan rolled his eyes. 'Shame I can't play it. It's got Mariah Carey on it. And that girl from *Neighbours* who had cancer.'

I couldn't speak after that. The pop starlet and my mother had had cancer at the same time. We followed her progress in the papers. But the starlet pulled through. She had a new album out and a new look. So much hair. You'd never believe she'd once been bald from chemo.

Anton came running up. He pointed to Dylan. 'Put that out, mate.'

Dylan pushed the burning end of the cigarette into his jeans, just above his knee. I squeaked in protest. 'Ow! Are you crazy?' In a fifties movie about white trash greasers, it would have been the ultimate tough guy move.

But it wasn't a movie and all Anton did was sigh and say, 'That's great, Dylan. Really clever.' Anton turned to me. 'I need a partner. You. In the canoe. Now.'

I shook my head. 'I can't swim.'

'She's keeping me company,' Dylan said. 'Hey. If she doesn't *want* to, she shouldn't *have* to.'

'It's okay,' I said. It didn't seem fair to have Dylan fighting my battles.

Anton looked me up and down, and his eyes were saying, *Fat girl, chicken, what are you – scared?* 'Have you got some kind of medical condition?' I shook my head. And now everyone was looking at me. Anton said, 'Go on – get your bathers.'

I stood up. 'I'm wearing them.' I had on boardies and my black skull halter. My skin was pink all over. I walked down the bank to the last canoe on the dock. Someone was making sound effects – the sound of a sumo wrestler thundering into the ring. Was it Richard? I couldn't tell. I gritted my teeth and kept walking.

'Ladies first,' Anton said.

I stepped in. The canoe jerked around and I stumbled.

'Whoa!' Bird laughed.

'Shut up!' I hissed, even though I knew he wasn't being nasty. Fleur on the other hand had nastiness up the arse.

As water splashed around my ankles I heard her gleeful shout, 'She's going to capsize!' I went to sit down, my face burning. I couldn't look at Dylan or Sarita.

I hated every Honeyeater, but most of all I hated Anton because the next thing he said was, 'You know, Fleur, it's a funny thing. Riley, hold onto the sides. On the count of three we're going over. One, two, THREE!'

The water was like ice, and it was heavy. When I first opened my eyes all I could see was black. I realised it was the bottom of the boat, and I was pressing up against it. I kicked, propelling myself under and out and swam up. I came out spluttering and heaving, with a constricted feeling in my throat, like I'd just swallowed a tennis ball. I hauled myself onto the dock and sat for a second, blinking at the campers, taking in their smiles and hearing their laughter through my waterlogged ears. Sarita was gesturing at me frantically. 'Riley!' she hissed. 'Your top!' I looked down to see that one of my boobs had escaped my halter. I rearranged my suit and made my face as blank as possible.

'Oh my God!' Fleur shrieked. 'How embarrassing.'

Anton threw me a towel. 'Great instincts, Riley.' For a second I thought he was talking about how I handled my wardrobe malfunction.

He addressed the Honeyeaters. 'What Riley did was she *used* the boat to launch herself out of danger. Like a platform, yeah?'

I wrapped the towel around my shoulders and started walking away.

'Riley?' Anton called. 'Where do you think you're going?'

I stuck my middle finger up at him and kept walking. Dylan was dozing, listening to something on his MP3. I could hear it enough to know it was hardcore – definitely not Mariah Carey. I pulled the white cord out of his left ear. 'Can I have some of that?'

He nodded and I sat down next to him and put the ear-plug in. He smiled and turned the volume up and the singer screamed and raged against an insane beat. I blocked my other ear with my hand and let the chaos in.

Healthy Animals

All the way back to camp I sat up the back of the mini-bus stewing. Fleur was snuggling up to Craig and she kept turning around in her seat to laugh at me. Now I really, really wanted to punch her. But worse than Fleur's flappy mouth were Sarita's sorrowful eyes – Sarita looking sorry for ME! I couldn't stand it. And Bird kept staring and then looking away. My boob-flash had him thrown into a world of sex and confusion, I was sure. Anton had given me a warning. I was supposed to tremble and quake when what I wanted to do was bitch-slap him to Christmas. What day was it? Tuesday? When was I leaving? Wednesday. Tomorrow! But tomorrow felt like a long way away.

Craig left Fleur to sit down next to me. He stretched his legs out and sighed and smiled. He said, 'Riley – '

'What?'

'Anton's a prick.'

'Wow – how'd you figure that?'

He laughed. 'You did really well though.'

'Yes. I flashed my boob.'

'Nothing wrong with that.' He looked at me. '*Really.*'

I stared at the back of the seat. I said, 'You're a little . . . liberal for one of God's children. What about setting a Christian example?'

'We're all God's children,' Craig said without a trace of irony. He grinned. 'I'm a healthy creature with a healthy appetite.'

Now we were sizing each other up. He looked at the yellow nicotine stains on my fingertips.

'Kissing a smoker is like kissing an ashtray.'

'Who's kissing?'

Craig looked over the seat. I followed his gaze. Fleur was staring at us with a face like thunder. The bus stopped and she jumped out of her seat and came straight for us.

'Here comes your girlfriend.'

'Aw, we're just hanging out.'

I started to say, 'Does she know that?' Then realised, I didn't care. I had two reasons to pursue Craig: one because he was hot, and two because Fleur thought he was hers. She was nearly on us when Craig nudged his shoulder into mine. 'You ever done it on a roundabout?'

I arched an eyebrow. 'Who hasn't?'

We smiled. We were both healthy creatures with healthy appetites.

Craig stood up, nodded at me. 'Laters.' He waltzed over to Fleur. She clutched his arm and glared at me.

I crossed my legs and felt my head to see if little red horns had grown.

THE TAIL OF A Q

Back at the smokers' bench – my spiritual home – I dreamed and dazed and painted my toenails seaweed green. Time was crawling. I consulted wristwatch and schedule. The Word was coming up. Scripture-based activities. Ugh. In the distance Roslyn was laying yoga mats in a circle under a tree. Most of the Honeyeaters had surfaced. I saw Dylan wheel in. He had his earplugs in; his face showed nothing. I ditched my cigarette and wandered over. Roslyn fairly pounced on me.

'Riley, isn't it?'

I nodded. Her hair fascinated me. It was piled on top of her head in a high ponytail, reminiscent of a date palm.

'Have you got your personal possession?'

'Sorry?'

Roslyn sighed. She took my arm and guided me away from the group. 'Didn't you read your program? We're playing a "Get to know you" game. I've asked everyone to bring a personal possession: something that says something about you. Sort of a show-and-tell, okay?'

I stared into her hair. There was life in there, I was sure. 'Why don't you run along to your cabin and pick something out? Ter-rif-ic.' She took a few steps backwards. 'I'd better – ' and she did the jazz hands as if to say that left unsupervised the Honeyeaters would start lighting fires or playing porno charades but all they were doing was lolling and talking. Everyone was sitting cross-legged, or with their legs curled up or stretched out in front of them – all except Dylan who was just out of the circle like the tail of a Q.

I opened my cabin door to a shriek. Sarita was standing by my bed. She whirled around and covered her throat with her hands. She looked so scared I almost laughed. And then I saw the flash of green between her fingers. She closed her eyes and moved her hand away. My sea-glass necklace glittered against her skin.

I stared at her, feeling my blood go hot. 'Take it off.'

'I was j-just – ' Sarita sputtered and struggled with the catch.

'My mother made me that necklace.' I practically spat the words. In the next few seconds my anger bounced from Sarita back onto myself, because I'd started something now. I'd opened the door, just a crack. I should have been more careful.

Sarita cowered by the bunk. 'It's beautiful.' She was babbling, buying time. 'Is she an artisan?'

'No. She just did a lot of short courses. She's dead.' I grabbed her arm. 'Turn.' I instructed. She obeyed. I was rough with her. I dug my finger into her neck as I lifted the catch. I gripped my necklace. 'What else did you take?'

'Nothing!' Sarita cried.

'Thief. Liar.'

I climbed the ladder to her bunk and started pushing through her things. It didn't take very long. She didn't seem to have any personal items. Even her wash-bag was free of fancy product – just a bottle of Pert and a toothbrush and toothpaste and some soap. Her limited wardrobe consisted of boring beige and lilac items with that hand-hewn vibe.

'Oh, nice!' I scoffed over a pair of granny-pants. 'Sensible *and* super-absorbent.' I threw them at her head and started prodding her pillow. My fingers closed on something sharp. I held up a small, jagged rock.

'Are you planning to stone me in my sleep?'

Sarita looked pained. 'It's my prayer rock.'

'What the fuck?'

'I put it in my pillow and when it hurts my head it reminds me to say my prayers.'

'Why do you need reminding?'

'Because I'm thinking of myself too much. I get caught up in what happened during the day and my problems and I forget.'

I jumped down from the bunk. 'Prayers don't work.' I put the rock in her palm. 'So is that your item?'

Sarita shook her head. 'It's not unique.' She clutched her rock in one hand. In the other she wrenched her granny-pants.

'Those are.'

I stood in front of the mirror and put my necklace on.

'It's really pretty,' Sarita ventured.

I grunted and started powdering my face. Sarita was like a mannequin in the background, still and indistinct. 'You know, magpies do that,' I told her. 'They steal shiny things. They look boring as fuck but they covet.'

'You swear a lot,' Sarita noted.

'I'm colourful.'

'I'm sorry about your mother. And I'm sorry about your necklace. I just wanted to see what it was like to wear something pretty. My mother calls jewellery the devil's baubles.'

'Jay-sus,' I laughed. 'My mother used to say that accessories were the only things that separated us from the animals.'

Sarita watched me make up in the mirror. Her eyes were sad and serious. She said, 'When I was ten I wanted to get my ears pierced. I pleaded and pleaded. My mother finally said yes, but instead of taking me to the chemist, she said she would perform the procedure herself with a leather-stitch needle.' Sarita hung her head. 'I never told anyone this. My parents wanted a boy only now my mother has had the hysterectomy and she hates me. I have no place in the world.'

I remembered. 'What about the shroud?'

'What do you mean?'

'Roslyn's shroud. You took it.'

Sarita was trying to keep her face straight but her chin was starting to wobble. ' I was going to give it back. And then

I thought maybe it would give me luck.' She hung her head. 'I'm so ashamed.'

She would have stayed standing that way forever if I hadn't grabbed her shoulders and given them a tight shake.

'Sarita,' I said. 'Sarita, you need to lighten up.' I went to my suitcase and pulled out a belt made of silver discs.

'Here,' I thrust it at her. 'Put this on. It's from *Mehico*.'

Sarita looked unsure. I frowned at her, so she knew I wasn't playing a trick, and she bit back a smile and put the belt around her waist.

'Wear it lower – it's supposed to sit on your hips.'

'Like that?'

'Exactly like that.'

Mum said, '*Sea-glass is special.*' It shouldn't be but it is. It's just broken glass: stubbies smashed at beach parties, fishermen's whisky left in the rocks, champagne cracked over ship's prows, missives flung from the starboard deck. It's just remnants buffed to infinity by a billion, trillion grains of sand, and you will never find two pieces of sea-glass that look the same. '*Riley, no one looks like you. No one is like you. You are unique.*'

Fatal Flaws

'My personal possession is this belt.' Sarita told the Honeyeaters. 'It's from my Mexican penpal, Paco. He's in prison in Juárez. He was caught trying to cross the border. His English is dire but he is an excellent silversmith.'

'*Bull!*' Richard coughed into his palm.

'In all honesty!' Sarita protested, blushing.

'Okay, and what does your personal possession say about you?' Roslyn coached.

Sarita held one of the silver discs in her fingers. She turned it over and said softly, 'It is not the kind of thing that I ever would have picked out for myself. But when I wear it I feel special. Like I have my soul on show, and it's all shiny, and intricate, and so it makes me feel like there's more to me than everyone thinks. That is all.' She hung her head and I could see beads of sweat on the top of her forehead.

Roslyn broke the silence. 'That's really beautiful.' She looked thrown by Sarita's response, and it was funny because I knew it wasn't true but at the same time, it was honest. 'Really . . . great. Riley?'

'Oh, I don't have anything,' I strung my little finger along my necklace. *Try making me talk, sister.*

I hadn't been the first person to foil Roslyn's party game. Dylan had been my inspiration. When Roslyn had called on him, he'd shaken some pills out of his vial and rolled them around his palm like diamonds. 'I call these my drifties,' he'd said. 'One gives you a kind of fuzzbox effect. Two make your eyelids feel like they're made out of cement. Three is the magic number. Three's when you start to drift away. After four, it depends on your tolerance. Start counting backwards from one hundred and see how far you get.' He squared his shoulders. 'Prescribed for pain relief. Street value – '

Craig cut him off, 'Thanks for the how-to. Real responsible.'

Dylan didn't respond. I started to wonder if maybe he hadn't taken a couple before coming to class. No one knew what to say, they were all just looking down, picking at their toenails, pushing dead leaves around the dirt.

Roslyn held her hand out. 'Let me see.'

Dylan tossed her the vial. She read the label and then tossed them back.

'Did you know I used to be a nurse?' Roslyn said smartly. Then her face softened. 'Dylan, you're not a wild boy. You don't have to pretend here. We're your friends.' Dylan went red. He shoved his vial back in his bag. Roslyn shook her head and looked to the clouds.

Now she was shaking her head at me.

'Really,' I insisted, 'I had a look and I don't have anything.'

Roslyn sighed. 'Riley, this is your time to tell us about yourself.'

'I just did.'

'Riley.'

I smiled. Roslyn started to say something then stopped. 'Fine,' she said. *Another bad apple.* She clapped her hands together. 'Who's next?'

Apart from outing Sarita's spin-ability, Roslyn's game held few surprises. Fleur's personal possession was a 'friendship ring' given to her by 'someone special' (she went all doe-eyed when she said it, but her toes were pointing straight at Craig); Lisa and Laura shared the same personal possession, a signed photograph of Del Covenant, Christian soul superstar (*To two special girls, PeaceLoveJesus, Del Covenant*); I felt sure Bird would say his binoculars, but he picked his trainers, he said he liked the lights because they made him feel calm; Richard's personal possession was a science fiction paperback called *The Mansions of Space*, ('It's about the hunt for the Shroud of Turin when it gets stolen in the twenty-fourth century'); and Ethan's was a Swiss Army knife which Roslyn promptly confiscated.

Craig went last. He took off his Youth Leader vest and shook his head a few times, looking at it with pride, and then he went into this unexpurgated ramble about him and Dylan and the good old days.

And I couldn't imagine them.

Craig ended with, 'It's so cool, looking over and seeing that Dylan has the vest too. I'm stoked. When we were twelve, we started this book where we wrote down all the Youth Leaders. Remember, D? We used to write their names, and everything about them – their attributes, what we could learn from them. Like, Mark Monroe could spot a bed-wetter at fifty paces but at the same time if you had a problem you could tell him and he wouldn't laugh at you, he'd just be straight up. And Dylan used to write their fatal flaws. You know, room for improvement.'

At this Ethan interrupted him. 'What's your fatal flaw?' It sounded more like an accusation than a question,

Craig stopped short. 'Shit. I don't know.'

'Language!' Roslyn interjected.

Then Bird spoke up – and Bird *never* spoke up. 'What's his?' he nodded to Dylan, but wouldn't look at him.

Dylan smiled a sad, flat smile and pointed to his legs.

The Word ended with 'meditation'. Roslyn had us all hold hands while she read from a little green book.

'This is just something to go away with:

A firemist and a planet,
A crystal and a cell;
A jellyfish and a saurian,
And caves where cave men dwell;
Then a sense of law and beauty,
A face turned from the clod –
Some call it Evolution,
And others call it God.'

The bell rang, and we all let go and wiped our hands. Roslyn said, 'God is behind everything. Behind the trees and the earth and the sea. That's pretty awesome, isn't it? I want you to think about this for tomorrow's discussion.'

I put my hand up. 'Roslyn?'

'Yes, Riley.'

'I call it Evolution.'

'Save it, Riley.'

Roslyn closed her little green book.

The Honeyeaters walked as a group to the mess hall for lunch. My silver belt gave Sarita a new swagger. I wondered what Dylan would make of it. She wasn't doing her usual head-down, stumble-bum wander, she was *sailing*. I was smiling at this when Richard and Ethan fell into step beside me. Ethan elbowed me in the side. 'You're going to *Hell*,' he said. Richard jabbed me in the other side. 'Slut.' They stormed off ahead. I was too stunned to respond. I stopped walking. I felt a tightness growing in my chest. I knew that feeling. It's the start of tears that never come. The first time I felt it was at Mum's funeral, when I couldn't cry. That was all hands on deck – everyone rubbing my back and going, 'I know, I know,' and 'It's okay,' and 'Let it out, love,' but no tears ever came. Call me Concrete Girl.

'Riley – are you okay?'

I looked up. Dylan was looking at me like I was a case.

'Fuck off.' I said it without thinking. He stared at me, then jammed his hands down on his wheels and shot off ahead.

FIELD RECORDINGS

After lunch, the Honeyeaters were told to assemble outside the rec room. I waited with Sarita. We leaned on the pinewood pole and listened to Neville attempting to coax some conversation out of Dylan.

'So,' Neville shook the arm of Dylan's chair. 'Big changes.' He paused for comic timing. 'Long hair.'

Dylan sniffed.

Neville adopted an exaggerated macho stance and gave his chair the once-over. 'What's your ride?' He was trying to be cool but Dylan wasn't having a bar of it.

'I could do with some of your hair,' he continued, touching his own head lightly. 'I don't know what God wants with mine but he seems intent on taking it.'

'Maybe you should get a hat.' Dylan sounded bored.

Neville considered this. 'I could,' he said. 'I could get a hat. Hats could become my thing. Everyone needs a thing, right?'

Dylan shrugged. There was a long silence.

'What about you?' Neville asked him. 'Are you into doing weights? If you are we've got some hand-weights, barbells . . . Bibles,' he joked.

Sarita poked me in the ribs. I saw Dylan's face close up. Fleur and Craig were approaching. They were walking in step, and looked like a shampoo commercial, all sun-kissed and leggy and happy. As soon as they saw Dylan they separated. Craig put his hand up for a high-five. Dylan ignored it, said something to Neville and then pushed off back to his cabin. After that no one seemed to know where to look except for Sarita who was staring at Craig with such longing that I had to snap my fingers in front of her face.

'We're going to do a trust walk,' Neville announced. He winked at me and put forth a shoebox. 'Pass these around, Riley.' I stared at the box, then my eyes moved up to his badge. He didn't need a hat – wacky badges were his thing. This one was black and white and basic. *I'm into Jesus,* it said. I passed the box around while Neville barked, 'Grab a blindfold and a partner.' At the sight of the usual suspects clutching to each other, Neville stressed, 'I want you to pair up with *someone you don't know very well.* Laura, Lisa, come on. Don't make me ask twice.'

I tried my blindfold on. It worked. I stood absolutely still and listened to the group get its thing together. Bird was humming, Laura and Lisa were pleading with Neville. I could hear shuffling and giggling. I was expecting Sarita to take my arm when I felt a column of warmth at my side. 'I saw this in a magazine once.' Craig's breath in my ear gave me the shivers. Two seconds later someone pinched my arm.

Fleur hissed, '*Sorry.*'

I heard Craig trying to appease her. 'But Fleur, I *know* you.' His voice had laughter behind it. Was he laughing at me or Fleur? It was impossible to know.

Neville's voice rang out. 'The game is leader/follower. The leader has to lead the follower around the camp. This is a non-verbal, non-visual experience. Use your senses to explore the world around you.'

Craig took my hand; sweaty. Nice.

He led me over the plain. I felt spidergrass tickling my bare ankles. Then we were in the scrub, and sticks snapped beneath my feet. I could feel the temperature change when we walked in and out of trees. I had a sense we were getting further away from the group. The idea of our seclusion made my temperature soar. The silence was claustrophobic. But it wasn't true silence – there was still activity and electricity in the air. It made me think of field recordings. I could hear: our footsteps on the hard ground; Craig's key-chain clinking; our breath out of sync; bird calls; insects rubbing their legs together; and all of this was weirdly sexy.

Craig stopped walking and dropped my hand. I felt him come behind me and push me forward. I panicked, thinking I was falling, but then my body bounced against a rope fence. Craig lifted my blindfold. 'Look down.'

I looked way down to a gaping hole in the ground. It looked like a giant's footstep. Or a natural well – only there was no water in there, just dry reddish mud decorated by crazed cracks and feral tracks.

'This is the crater,' Craig said. 'Legend has it this is where the European settlers threw the bodies after they massacred the Aborigines. The mud is red because of the blood. Cool, isn't it?'

'Is this where you take all your girls?'

Craig nodded. 'When we were Bronzewings, Sarita fell down here. I was the one who found her. I tied a rope to that tree, tied the other end around my waist, abseiled down, put her over my shoulder and pulled us both up. Awesome.'

I looked around. 'I thought we were supposed to be non-verbal.'

There, at the edge of something vast and ancient, Craig lurched forward and kissed me. It wasn't a sweet kiss. His lips felt rubbery. He pulled back and stared at me. 'Will you meet me tonight? Midnight?'

'Where?'

'At the roundabout.'

'Okay.'

Craig turned. In the sharp sunlight his profile was perfect, he had what Chloe would call Greek God-ness – then a shadow fell and a sly look entered his eyes and I had a sudden paranoid flash that he might push me and I would become part of the legend.

I put that thought out of my head and stayed still as he put my blindfold back on and led me back to the group.

THE GEEK SHALL INHERIT THE EARTH

Dinner.

The Honeyeaters' table was getting elbow-roomy. Fleur and Craig were sitting with the counsellors. Bird had permission to observe the fairy wrens nest-building by the recycling cage. Dylan still hadn't surfaced. I pictured him flaking out in his cabin, watching the dust motes dance in the sun's fading rays. Sarita was too excited to eat. She pushed her tray aside and whispered, 'What was it like being partnered with Craig?' She looked from me to Fleur, as if trying to gauge when the catfight was going to break out.

'It was okay.'

'But what did you talk about?'

'Nothing. It was non-verbal, remember?'

'He's perfect,' Sarita sighed.

'He's *okay*.' I was outwardly cool but on the inside my heart was racing.

Everyone else was talking about Dylan.

'It was a surfing accident,' Richard was saying. 'He came off the board and slammed into a sandbank.'

'He doesn't look like a surfer,' Laura said.

'He looks scary,' Lisa said. 'What's with all the black?'

'You'd look pretty scary if you'd lost the use of your legs,' Richard paused and nodded down to his groin. 'And the rest.'

The twins went, 'Eww.'

'I wonder if he has a colostomy bag,' Ethan mused.

Richard sniffed. 'Of course he does, idiot.'

I leaned over the table. 'Do you think Dylan would like to hear you all discussing him like he's some sort of freak?'

'What's it to you?' Richard asked.

'Unh!' I made a face. 'It's rude, is what. And I'm eating. You people are weird. You've all been coming here for years – '

'We haven't,' Lisa and Laura chirped.

'Okay, but they have.' I pointed to Richard and Ethan. I was trying to work out the group dynamic, if there was one. 'I don't get it. Isn't Dylan your friend? Aren't you all friends?' The boys exchanged a glance. I figured they'd made a pact not to speak to me because I was contaminated, but the urge to gossip was too tasty.

Richard said, 'Thing is, Dylan used to be a bully.'

'He was a tool,' Ethan confirmed.

'Is this true?' I asked Sarita. She nodded. 'He was very competitive. He and Craig – '

'They thought they were rock stars,' Richard cut in. 'You might call it hubris.' He held his fork aloft and smiled for a long time, and when I didn't smile back he licked his lips nervously and looked away.

'You really believe that, don't you?' I said. 'That God's got a plan for everyone. No bad deed goes unpunished. The geek shall inherit the earth. You think bad things don't happen to good people? Wake up, Australia! Read the fucking paper.'

Richard put his hands over his ears. As soon as Ethan saw this he did the same. They both closed their eyes and started chanting. 'My God is a good God, is a just God, is the One True Holy Father.' La, la, *la*.

'You're idiots.' I spooned some mudcake into my mouth. 'My God is chocolate,' I said to Sarita, but she didn't laugh, she just looked worried.

I missed Chloe.

I ditched theatre sports in favour of a long shower. I washed my hair and used a come-hithery body spray. I put my jeans back on, and my best bra, and a peasant blouse that gave me coverage without being a total sack. Then I lay in bed looking at the pictures in my bunker book. They were beautiful, but they were a lie. In my world you didn't see bright-eyed children with sparrows on their shoulders any more than you saw pots of gold at the end of the rainbow. My world was about white fat rolling over my waistband, guys with glazed eyes, girls on buses, at the beach, at the mall, whispering, laughing, bitching. Drinking shots with Chloe in the park until I couldn't tell the difference between up and down. Dad's look of disappointment. Random days when I felt most hollow, I'd sit by Mum's grave and watch the ants make a matrix on her headstone.

I was too wired to sleep, so I started to read and by the time Sarita came back I was engrossed.

'What are you reading?' she asked.

'*Utopia*.' I put the cover down and gave her my report. 'It's about a made-up society where the inhabitants live in perfect harmony. There's no crime or personal possessions and everyone practises "religious tolerance" – which means you can follow whatever God you want but you can't rag on anyone about who they choose.'

Sarita was looking confused. 'But there's only one God.'

'You're sure about that?'

'Certain.'

'Well, you're lucky,' I said. *Safe*, I thought.

According to the introduction, Thomas More said *Utopia* was a satire because if he'd called it a manifesto he would have been killed. And then he got killed anyway for disagreeing with Henry VIII, the bastard king. The intro also said that *Utopia* started a whole new genre. I like it because the reader can't not compare the imagined world with his own world and wonder about how things could change. And change – or the possibility of it – is the only reason we don't all jump sixteen floors.

I thought about Spirit Ranch. How it was supposed to be some kind of Utopia, but actually Chloe's prison call was closer to the mark. We had our nametags, our privileges removed, and too many boundaries. I took the thought down a dark alley: If this was a prison, then who was top dog? And just as I was thinking this, Fleur came in with fucky hair and her blouse buttoned up the wrong way.

I looked at her. She stared back accusingly. She shook her head and let out an explosive, 'Slut!'

I just laughed. 'Careful,' I said under my breath. 'Don't get me started.'

IN THE THICK

At 11.30 pm I lay in bed, fully dressed, listening to Fleur and Sarita's sleep-harmonics and staring at the crack between the curtains. Outside, the plain looked like a CCTV crime-scene waiting to happen. I had watched the cabin lights go out until all that remained were two flickering bars – one outside the shower block, the other outside the counsellors' annexe.

Fleur snored. I shined the torch on her sleeping form. She looked like a model in a sleepwear catalogue, she had the whole kit: sleep-mask, earplugs, Country Road pyjamas and her long hair cascading down her no-tangles satin pillow. The only dint in perfection was the soundtrack. Fleur's snoring was not the soft purr of a Rolls Royce; it was more like the cheap outburst of a two-stroke engine. I liked thinking that there was something she couldn't control. It felt like ammunition.

Suddenly Sarita spoke. Or rather, she snapped. She didn't sound like herself. Her sleeptalking voice had big balls.

'No . . . Because. God! Just shut up, Mum. Shut Up. You don't know anything.'

I trailed her with the torch. Sarita was frowning and her hand was curled around her prayer rock. I liked Sarita. I felt a little guilty that I was about to get off with her crush. I didn't feel bad for Fleur's sake – just Sarita's. But she was dreaming if she thought she had a chance with Craig, and hadn't I just that morning vowed to live adventurously and fling my whole soul into everything I did? I had. I would. Nothing could stop me.

I left at five minutes to midnight. In my bag I had lipgloss, ciggies, breathmints, a sarong and an emergency condom, brand – Gigantor. (Chloe and I had purchased the packet online using Norma's credit card. We laughed, we mimed; we imagined the worst. *Gigantors! Not for the Easily Intimidated!* They were gherkin-sized and kind of oily . . .)

Outside the air was crisp and smelled like smoked sap. There were so many stars that the sky looked like a fabulous sequinned quilt. I rubbed my goosebumpy arms as I ran through the plain, past the showers, down the track. There was a light glowing from the garage, and I crept in. 'Hellooo,' I whispered, scanning for Craig. 'Hey Youth Leader. Hey Loverboy!'

Nothing. Just the hissing of the kerosene lamp.

I went out to the roundabout, sarong-ed my shoulders, smoked a cigarette or three and waited.

Waiting is an art form at which I excel. The trick of it is to keep your mind occupied. I thought about sex – tumbling, Choe and I called it. I thought about how once you start you can't go back. How sometimes – most of the time if I was honest – I wished I could go back. I liked the idea that each new encounter effaced the last one. But if this were really true then my memory of said tumbles would be gone too. The first guy I ever slept with was Aaron Becker. His dad had a caravan dealership, and we did it in a different one every day of the Easter break. Foreplay was if he folded the bed down. During the act, Aaron would stare above my head, and I'd stare at his mouth moving. After a while I figured out he was counting. Counting! Like I was exercise.

'What did you get?' I asked him the last time.

'What?'

'How many reps? . . . I counted eleven.'

He looked at me like he hated me. He said, 'You're really weird, you know that?' And he tied a knot in the condom and tucked it behind the mini fire extinguisher where it wouldn't be found until Darwin or never.

Craig appeared in front of me. He was silent and smiling like an apparition, a bush ghost I'd dreamed into existence. I felt that if I touched him my hand would go right through his skin and all I'd get was air. He took two cans of VB from his backpack, cracked one and passed it to me. I took a sip. *This is real*, I thought. And, *Yuck. Stolen beer is warm beer.*

'Where did you score these?'

'Storeroom.'

'Youth Leader privilege?'

He laughed shortly. 'Yeah.'

Without preamble, Craig lunged. It was a sloppy kiss, but not without promise. I lay back. He kissed me harder, and moved over me until his chest was firm against mine.

One hand was on the back of my head; the other was working my button fly. The roundabout shifted east and my top half went with it. The rest of me was pinned down by Craig's thigh. He stopped. He grabbed the waist of my jeans and yanked them down. He always had a hand on me, and I almost made a joke about him being used to girls trying to bolt – but in the thick is no place for jokes, so I just concentrated on his perfect face.

Craig pulled his jeans down with his other hand.

'Wait,' I said. 'Aren't you going to use something?'

'Yeah, whatever.'

I reached behind for my bag. 'I've got one. Hold on – '

Craig's breath was hot on my face, 'I don't do condoms.'

'Stop,' I said.

He stopped. 'Why?' he sounded irritated, worse than that, bored.

'You *have* to do condoms.'

'I'm clean.' He said. 'I'll pull out.'

I sat up. 'No you won't because you're not even getting *in*.'

Craig sighed. He heaved off me and kicked his feet in the sand. He seemed to be brooding. Finally he turned to me. 'You could – '

'*What?*' I hissed.

'Finish me off with your hand?' And then when it was obvious that *that* wasn't going to happen, he shrugged. 'Your loss.'

I stared at him. I *hated* him! He wasn't worth my emergency condom. He wasn't worth spit. My top was up, my jeans were down, all my necessaries trembled under the stars. I started the awkward process of getting back into my clothes while he tapped his finger on his tinnie. He took a sip and burped.

'Nice,' I said.

'What's wrong with you?'

'If you don't know I'm not going to tell you.'

'You have the best tits,' Craig went for them but I moved away.

'Creep.'

WILDLIFE

I didn't feel like going back to camp. I guess Craig didn't either – tumble or no tumble he had a six-pack to finish. I sat, smoked and stared up. Now the sky looked like a colossal bruise. I watched the clouds roll across it, migrating at first in tight huddles then breaking up, stretching out.

'Look at the clouds . . .' I said, mostly to myself.

Craig cracked a dint in his tinnie.

'They look like renegades. They're moving so fast.'

Craig looked up. His features twisted into a question mark. It seemed like he was searching for something. 'It's going to rain,' he said finally.

There was a rustle in the nearby bushes.

'What was that?'

'Wildlife,' Craig said. 'It's probably a wombat.' His hands were hovering above my stomach. He poked it and made blubbery noises.

'Hey!' I smacked his hand away. 'Don't be mean.'

He laughed. From the bushes someone laughed back.

Craig stood up. 'Who's that?'

'Who's that?' the voice echoed. And I only had to hear it once to know it was Bird. He laughed again, a dumb, honking sound, and then he came forward. 'I saw you,' he said. His eyebrows bounced up and up and up.

'What did you see?' Craig's tone was murderous but Bird didn't get it.

He covered his eyes with his hands. 'I saw SEX.'

Craig shoved him. The action was so swift that if it hadn't been for the thud of Bird hitting the bar and falling to the floor of the roundabout I would have missed it. I watched, stunned, as Bird curled into a ball. He looked like he was trying to compress himself. He opened his mouth and –

He sounded like windscreen wipers when there's no water.

He sounded like a sword coming out of a wound.

Craig stood over him. 'You didn't see *anything*.' He picked up his beer. His face was fixed between a grimace and a smile.

'What's wrong with you?' I shouted. 'Are you a caveman?'

'He's a little perve.'

'He's . . . look at him!' I crouched down next to Bird and put my hands on his shoulders. I pressed softly, said, 'shhh, shhh' until his shriek dissolved into a broken croaky hum.

'You'd better get someone,' I told Craig.

'He's all right. He always has these fit things. Give him five.'

'I thought you were the Youth Leader,' I muttered. 'He needs help.'

Craig stared from Bird to me, to the horizon. Then he drained his beer and turfed it. 'You help him.' He walked off with his hands in his pockets, not quite whistling, but almost.

I sat with Bird until his 'fit-thing' was over. But we didn't go back straight away. For a long time, maybe half an hour, we watched a spider spin her web. Spiders usually make me shriek and flap but seeing this one silently work her silver threads seemed like a privilege. I'd never really given 'nature' much thought, but at that moment I wondered how human beings and all their dumb lumbering could have any place in the world.

'People are idiots,' I said to Bird.

A strange, sad sound surfaced.

Bird sat up straight. 'That's the Southern Boobook Owl.' He turned on the twitch. '*Ninox novaeseelandiae*. The smallest and most common owl in Australia. Breeds in October – '

I put my hand on his arm. 'Owls are sad.' And then I told him the fable about the owls of Athens. 'The owls used to sing beautifully, so beautifully that they deemed themselves kings and decided that all the other animals should lay treasures and riches at their feet. One night the moon asked them, "Why do you think you deserve this?" and the owls said, "Because we have the loveliest song." So the moon used her magic to give the owls' voices to the nightingales – and all the owls had left was a haunted, *Whoo Whoo*.'

Bird said, 'Actually, it's more like a *mo-poke*.' Bird called – his voice was high and distinctive, and the Boobook echoed him. He nodded and continued. 'Or *more-pork*. Some clowns call it the more-pork owl.'

'I like my story better,' I said. 'My story has pathos.'

The Boobook's song of regret followed us back to camp. The night was getting fierce. The sky was dark and the air felt heavier. We walked faster, as thunder clapped above our heads. At goodbye Bird grabbed my hand and squeezed it. I understood that I had him for life.

IT IS ALL GOOD

'Riley!' Sarita whispered, not two seconds after I'd crept in the door.

She was beaming at me.

'You really DO sleepwalk! Quick, check your feet.'

'Why?'

'There might be clues as to where you wandered.'

'I'm not asleep,' I said. 'I haven't been . . . I'm awake.'

Sarita studied my face. 'Did you go to see Dylan?'

'No. Why would I see Dylan?'

'Isn't he your intended?'

'My *intended*?'

'You know, Romance?'

'Sarita. You're very weird. And I'm tired.'

Fleur let out a titanic snore. Sarita ducked her head under her covers and came up smiling. 'I saw once in an American movie they replaced a girl's hair mousse with a depilatory cream. It's a good one, no? But I think perhaps the smell would give it away.'

'I thought Fleur was your friend.'

'Fleur is NOT my friend. You know that Poppy, the girl whose bed you took? Last year, she and Fleur put shit in my bed.'

'What kind of shit?'

'*Shit* shit.' Sarita nodded solemnly. 'It is all good. You cannot scare a shrewd person with small provocation.'

I smiled. I liked the way Sarita buggered up common slang. *It's all good*. People said that all the time. They said it when they'd spilt their drink, or when their parents got divorced. They said it like nothing bad was ever supposed to happen. Like being upset was un-Australian or something.

I suddenly noticed Sarita's hair. In the lamplight, free from its plaits, it looked lustrous, even glamorous.

'Your hair looks good like that,' I told her.

She patted her head self-consciously. 'There's too much of it.'

'You just need to rein it in.' I yawned. 'We'll work on it tomorrow. Right now, I need to sleep.'

'You are a true friend, Riley.'

Sarita's words floated down from the bunk and pressed into me.

Not, I said in my head. *You wouldn't say that if you knew where I'd been for the last two hours.* I felt hot with guilt again. Then I reasoned that Craig turned out to be a pig's ear – so really, I'd done her a favour.

Did that make me a true friend?

Can you even be a true friend after two days?

It was too hot. I ditched my sheet and rolled onto my other side and tried to push the lumps out of my pillow. I remembered where I was. I remembered Wednesday. I remembered that I didn't need creepy Christian camp friends and I stopped thinking about it. The rain hammered down. To get myself to sleep I thought about the crater. How much rain would it take to fill it? I imagined that when it was full the water would be red and thick with stuff. All of the crater's secrets would come to the surface, ancient bones floating on their backs like a pregnant woman in a saltwater pool.

ON THE THIRD DAY

SPIRITUAL DEVELOPMENT

In my dream Craig had killed Bird. He was sprawled on the roundabout with a dumbfuck expression on his face, going around and around and around. I told Craig we should take his trainers off – because dead boys don't need shoes. But when I touched Bird's foot the lights on his trainers started flashing, and his eyes went *ping* – open.

As did mine. On cue, the PA started its squeal and clank. Roslyn boomed into space like a big friendly giant.

'Attention campers. This is your morning thought: *Let us cleanse ourselves from everything that contaminates either flesh or spirit.*'

Yes, let's. I groaned, rolled over and went back to sleep.

When I woke again the cabin was empty. It was raining outside and the humidity made the air smell sour. I stretched my arms, 'Wednesday!' I reached for *Utopia*. My bus ticket peeked between the pages, a seemingly innocuous bookmark that said in fourteen hours I would be on my way to Chloe and Ben Seb's party; to fun and freedom and other good things that start with F. But right now it was shower time. I gathered my stuff and bolted across the rain-drenched plain.

The water pressure was non-existent. I stood under the lame dribble for longer than my allotted three minutes. I was thinking about Craig, replaying The Arrival: his sleepy smile, his eyes staying on me as he handed me a beer. We both knew what was about to happen. There was the crackle of electricity, the pop of the tinnie – my stomach lurching like oil in a lava lamp – but I couldn't hide from the bitter end: Craig the cad laughing at me, Bird whimpering on the roundabout floor. I wondered if Craig was going to acknowledge me, if Bird had blurted anything. I wanted to scoop them up: *what say the three of us just call last night a bad dream?*

I stepped out of the shower but when I went to get dressed I realised my towel and clothes had disappeared. It didn't take long for the ramifications of this to sink in. After a few cold minutes, I heard somebody walk into the block. I stood on the bench and peered over the door. It was Janey, Olive's psycho-tweenie enemy. 'Hey – ' I tried not to smile too desperately. 'Someone's nicked my clothes. Can you –' She ran out, looking scared. I could hear the sound of activity outside. Campers were jumping puddles, and shrieking and getting loose. I climbed back on the bench and scouted for lost property but all I could see was a sodden scrunchie. I sat. I thought about how to approach this. I figured I had two options – wait or bolt. *What would Chloe do?*

Chloe would go frisking out into the open. I was not

Chloe. I gave pretty good about owning my fatness, I could dress provocatively, and I only sucked my stomach in when I was squeezing past someone but for all my boldness I'd never actually showed myself to anyone – not completely. And I wasn't about to do it now.

So I waited. When all was quiet outside, and I'd determined that the campers had gone in for grub, I opened the shower door. I tiptoed over the cold floor and attached myself to the breezeblock entrance. I peered through one of the holes. It looked all clear. I took a deep breath. Just as I was about to run I saw something in the corner of my eye. It was Dylan. He was heading for his cabin. I decided to chance it.

'Hey!' I yelled.

He stopped. I saw his elbows working. He wheeled around slowly.

Dylan could only see my head, but he quickly worked out what was going on.

'Nudie run?' he inquired.

'Someone stole my clothes.'

He nodded, and looked at me with a half-smile, a look that said, *I know*.

'Could you get me a towel or something?'

Dylan looked around. He shot over to the flagpole. He used his crutches to get to the rope and then he pulled the camp flag down. He came back to me and held it out with his eyes closed. I snatched the flag and ran back into the toilets, where I arranged it like a sarong. When I went back to say thank you, Dylan had already gone. Damn! He was fast!

Back in cabin three I slipped out of the flag and into my goodbye dress – a Goth Lolita number with snake-y sleeves. I put on black lace leggings and ankle boots so pointy they should have come with a licence. I looked in the mirror. 'Wednesday you big, gorgeous, beautiful thing. I never thought we'd make it.' I put on too much dead-red lipstick, drew a satanic star on Fleur's pillow, and then I walked through the drizzle to breakfast, undaunted.

A Pig's Ear

I suspected Fleur was the clothes-thief. The look on her face when I walked into the mess hall confirmed it. She was smirking. She'd obviously told. The Honeyeaters were all staring at me. Staring and whispering, the creeps. I hovered in front of the servery, shaking the rain out of my violet hair. I wrung out my sleeves, and bent over like Chloe doing the Downward Dog. Raindrops whitened the muddy tiles. I saw an upside-down Olive backing into the kitchen, loaded up with trays. A minute later she was standing in front of me, wiping her hands on her apron.

'There's only Weet-Bix left,' she said. 'It's gone all crumby.'

'Bring it on,' I held up my bowl. 'How are the psycho-tweenies?'

'They leave me alone now. They think you're scary.'

Me?' I laughed. I turned around. 'Janey and that' were watching me with their mouths agape. I laughed again, this time *evilly.* I winked at Olive. 'Tell them in my spare time I bite the heads off chickens.'

She nodded and said in a rush, 'There're biscuits in the back – do you want some? I think you're an angel sent here by God for me and Bird. He told me what you did. No one's ever looked out for us before. Bird used to cop it heaps bad. One year they scratched up his binoculars. That was the pair he got from Dad. They don't make them like that any-more. That's what Mum said.' She smiled anxiously. 'I'll get the biscuits.'

I tried to imagine 'Janey and that' as the camp threat but couldn't see it.

I took my tray over to the Honeyeaters' table. The twins gave me bright, fake smiles. 'Don't get up,' I said.

'Long shower?' Fleur inquired.

'Don't,' I warned her.

The space next to Sarita – my seat – was laden with dirty plates, burnt bits of toast, eggshells and soggy Weet-bix. Sarita made no effort to move the mess.

'Hello?' I nudged her. 'What's up with you?'

She didn't respond. I panned the table. Fleur was smiling superciliously, and buttering her toast with jaunty dash-like strokes. Bird was easier to read, he had his head low, but his eyes were racing. *Something was up.*

'What have I done?' I asked in a bored tone. I hoped it sounded like I was joking.

'So,' Fleur announced. 'Craig told us that you tried to make him . . . you know.'

'What?'

'Have sex with him.'

I took a step back, incredulous. '*What?*'

She shrugged and took a bite of toast. I rankled from top to toe. First of all it was bullshit, and secondly, it was stupid and insulting, and so not worth it. Craig was at the counsellors' table. His eyes met mine for a millisecond. A smirk started to form but then he must have reconsidered because his face snapped back to being beautifully blank.

I scratched my arm and looked back to the table. 'Yeah, that's right. I attacked him in a fit of lust.' I fluttered my eyes accordingly. 'It was . . . unbelievable.'

Bird spluttered – more of a spasm than a laugh – and a fine spray of yoghurt landed on the table in front of him. He wiped the smeary table with a hanky.

Fleur said, 'It's a commonly known fact that girls with over-eating issues become sexually active earlier than their slimmer counterparts.'

'Fuck off.'

'Just because *you* think you're special doesn't mean anyone else does.'

Bird suddenly stood up and stuttered, 'L-l-leave her alone!'

'Thank you.' I shook my hair. But I was feeling less brave than I looked. My knees had given a little. I had to get out of there. I looked at Sarita – why didn't she defend me?

Fleur persisted with her character assassination. 'I suppose you're after Bird too?' She shook her head. 'You're sick.'

'She's probably a sex addict.'

'She boob-boozled him,' Richard cackled. Ethan cracked up with him, and even the twins were giggling. Then Sarita stood up and walked away and I was startled at how much that felt like a hit. I wanted to run after her. 'He was a pig's ear,' I wanted to shout, 'a pig's ear!' Instead, I shoved my tray down. 'I didn't make Craig do anything. I wouldn't touch him with a *crane*.'

Fleur looked around the table, blinking. 'Did you hear something?'

'A lost soul,' Ethan said solemnly.

Richard nodded. 'A dead person.'

I stormed out.

WHEELCHAIR 101

Outside it was Niagara-ish. I hadn't realised I was going to
see Dylan until I was standing outside his door, at the end
of the pine ramp. I knocked. He opened the door and silently
let me in. Inside the furniture was fixed low. When I sat on
the bed, I misjudged the distance and nearly smashed my
chin to my knee. I tried to save face by pointing to the
barbells – 'Neville?'

Dylan rolled his eyes. There was a hoist above the bed.
I resisted the urge to yank it. I could see his bathroom
through the open door. There was a chair in the shower
and rails, lots of rails. I felt a bit queasy looking at Dylan's
'conveniences' so I fixed my gaze on his mudflaps.

'Did you make those?'

'Yeah. I was trying to be offensive. But most people don't
look down that far.' Dylan brought a jar full of dead
cigarette ends out of his top drawer. Then he offered me
his packet.

'It's okay,' he said. 'They won't come in here.'

'I don't care if they do.' I turned to him and stole his line.

'Match me.' He smiled and I tried to smile back, but I wasn't convincing.

Dylan said, 'It's no use crying over Youth Leader Craig.'

'How do you know?'

Dylan held his cigarette between his thumb and forefinger like a WW2 fighter pilot and took a neat puff. 'I'm observant. I don't have as many distractions as you able-bodied folk.'

'Is that what you call us?' I was happy to change the subject. 'No, I'm serious – is there like a group name?'

'Mostly *normal*.'

'What do you call yourselves?' I blushed. I felt like I was saying wrong thing after wrong thing but it was better than talking about Craig.

'Crips. I believe the collective is "a chaos of crips". But *you* can't call me that. That'd be like a white guy calling a black guy "nigga" – not cool.'

'Seriously?'

'No.' Dylan made a face. 'There was this guy at the rehab – Ross – he called us Mutards – a cross between mutants and retards. He used to do comics like, *Zombie Mutards from Hell will Rise Again and Steal your Limbs*.'

I laughed. 'Cool.'

Dylan went on, 'Ross was dead from the waist down. That's the charm of rehab – there's always someone worse off than you. Except maybe Alice. She couldn't move anything. Well – her head. She had a sign on the back of her chair that said "My mind is a castle". She did paintings by holding a brush in her mouth. Portraits. Only you could never tell who the subject was.' He chuckled and gave me a reconstruction of events. 'She'd go, "It's Don." "Who?" "Don!" "I don't see it." "You're all philistines! Philistines!"'

'What's it like – ' I stopped, mesmerised by the notches on Dylan's chair.

Dylan studied me. 'You want to ask me what it's like to have all this . . .' he looked down at his legs, '. . . useless beauty.'

'Forget it,' I said. 'It's a stupid question.'

'Go ahead.'

I took a breath. 'Okay. What's it like being in a wheelchair?'

'It's kind of like being invisible. But it has its perks.' Dylan reached behind his back and pulled out a hipflask. He took a sip and then passed it to me. 'The chair hides a multitude of sins.'

I sipped from the flask. The whisky burned my throat.

Dylan was drunk! It had happened quickly. I'd heard more out of him in twenty minutes than the whole time I'd been at camp. He was leaning forward in his chair and waving his hands about. 'Wheelchair 101. This is what you learn – people are either starers or avoiders, and your body always betrays you.' He hunched down and fixed me with a firm gaze. 'I'll tell you a story: The first time I went Out-out the Leisure Officer arranged for a group of us Mutards to go see a movie. It was Tight Tuesday so the place was packed. We had to use a lift to get to the cinema but it could only fit us one at a time. It was like being in a dunk box. Like "don't look down" unless you want to see pity-city. I fucking hate that. We wheeled in single file and there was this kid eating his popcorn and watching us like *we* were the movie. Duncan was in front of me. He's C6 – when he was twelve he fell under the train he was tagging. Anyway, he's twenty-something now, and he's hard, plays wheelchair rugby, has a neck like a bull's, but under that kid's stare his neck went brick-red.' Dylan shrugged. 'In the end it doesn't matter what front you present. The body betrays you and people are either starers or avoiders.'

We were quiet. I didn't dare look at Dylan in case my face betrayed what I was thinking.

'Are you feeling sorry for me?' Dylan asked.

I shook my head, and I forced myself to look at him.

'You want another observation?' he asked.

'Okay.'

'Fleur doesn't wear underpants.'

'Fleur goes commando?'

'Yes indeed.' Dylan smiled.

'How do you know?'

'Let's just say I have a vantage point.'

'That's gross.'

I felt annoyed that Dylan was so schooled on Fleur's pink bits.

'Fleur snores,' I told him.

He stopped smiling. 'Really?'

'Like a diesel in distress. And she farts in her sleep.' He looked so dashed by this that I forgot all about pity and ripped into him. 'What is it with you guys? She's so boring. She's not *that* hot. She looks like a prototype. And she's a bitch.'

Dylan mumbled, 'Well, I don't know about that.'

'Has she even talked to you?' He went red. Things had gotten too personal. I back-pedalled. 'It's none of my business. I just hate the way girls like her get away with shit and still get adored. It's just . . . wrong. The world is wrong.'

'Gee, you think?' Dylan scowled. He was looking at me differently now, like he hated me a little and all because I'd told a truth. I pictured us butting heads – loser to loser – tragic to tragic – Mutard to Mutard.

'Funny,' I said. 'We're sort of in the same boat.'

'It's not funny,' Dylan said. 'It's pathetic.' His face went choke-like. 'I have to change my bag.' Then he laughed. 'I'm joking. You should have seen the look on your face. It's okay, Riley, I don't have a shit-bag. I can wipe my own arse and everything.'

He started trying to get out of his chair. He was using his crutches but floundering. 'What are you doing?' I asked. 'Do you need – '

He cut me off with his hand. 'No.'

'Why are you mad at me?' I muttered, just loud enough for him to hear.

Dylan rubbed the heel of his hand on his forehead. 'Because. Because you don't know what I'm capable of. You all think I'm . . . forget it.'

I stood up. 'I'm going to go.'

'Good. Go back to . . . wherever.'

I left, feeling a kind of wrenching in my stomach. I was at the end of the ramp when I heard a crash. I raced back. Dylan was on the floor and his chair was on its side.

It was awful. His face was aflame and he wouldn't look up and I didn't know what to do. I righted his chair (it was lighter than I thought it would be). I found his crutches and held them up. He shook me away. He put his palms down flat and scuttled backwards until his back was against his bed. He pulled himself up onto the bed. And then just sat staring at the chair, puffing.

He pushed the hoist and we watched it swing back and forth like a pendulum. Dylan started slowly. 'My therapist wasn't sure about my coming back here. He's cool. I've had him since the hospital. He said, "I'm not going to feed you shit and call it chocolate cake . . . Nothing's ever going to be the same again." I told him the doctors hadn't ruled out that I might walk again and he goes, "Meanwhile, there's the chair, you have to learn to work it, baby. Because the chair can be your best friend or your worst enemy."'

Dylan smiled. It was the first time I'd noticed his teeth. They were small and white and neat, like baby teeth. 'He seriously called me "baby" like some kind of Hollywood producer – while everyone else was just tiptoeing around me asking what I wanted from the vending machine.' He looked at me, his face full of lost-ness. 'I don't know what I'm doing here.'

'Me either,' I said.

Dylan looked away. 'It's shit.'

'I know.'

PERIOD OF ADJUSTMENT

I decided to try to phone Chloe. I wanted something normal. I wanted her to remind me that as soon as I was out of here none of this would mean anything. Through the rec room windows I could see the teeming mass of campers. They had energy to burn and nowhere to burn it. They looked like a rodeo. Roslyn was calling a vote – who wanted indoor Nerfball? Who wanted Statues? Who wanted Trust Fall? Hands shot up at the last suggestion. The rules of Trust Fall had been imparted to me via Sarita during one of her early information floods: Campers gather in two lines facing each other. They then lift a member of the group and pass him or her above their heads all the way down the line. Campers are supposed to come out of Trust Fall with a renewed sense of trust for their compatriots. I couldn't see myself coming out of it with anything but concussion.

I watched for a while and then I walked around the building to Counsellor Neville's office. His door was half-open. The smell of fresh-brewed coffee wafted out. I could hear mumbles and movement. Then silence. He called out, 'Is someone there?'

I made my appearance.

Counsellor Neville looked relaxed. He wasn't sitting behind his desk; he was resting his bum on the edge. He was tie-less and his shirt was unbuttoned to reveal a few ginger hairs fighting for his throat.

'Riley Rose,' he announced.

There was a man standing with his back to us, studying the camp photos. He was wearing the traditional khaki ranger's garb, rain-spattered. He turned around and smiled broadly. His teeth were blindingly white against his dark skin. He said, 'G'day.'

'Hi.'

'This is Trevor Green,' Neville said, 'Trevor works with Parks and Wildlife. His great-grandfather was a Wotjobaluk elder. He knows the desert like the back of his hand. We've brought Trevor in to enlighten you all about natural history. Did you bring your slides, Trev?'

Trevor nodded, 'Heaps.' He jerked his head. 'In the you-beaut.'

Even though I was in the room, it didn't feel like this conversation was happening for my benefit. Trevor was smiling at Neville in a steady, unnerving manner – and it seemed like Neville was tasting his words before he spoke. The good counsellor kept looking like he was about to smile, but then he'd frown at the carpet. I studied the photos again. Neville moved to the business side of his desk and shuffled some papers. Trevor put his hat back on. 'Righto. I'll get those slides.'

'What can I do for you, Riley?' Neville asked.

'Can I make a phone call? It's important.'

'What's the emergency?'

'It's not an emergency, it's just – ' I was tired. My mind was mush. All I could come up with was: 'It's my best friend's birthday.'

'If I let you make a phone call then everyone else will want to make a phone call.' He shook his head. 'Sorry, Riley, I can't allow it.'

'What's so wrong with people wanting to communicate?'

Neville laughed. 'There's nothing wrong with wanting to communicate. I think you'll find we encourage it. We're all about being open, Riley.' He stood and straightened one of the pictures on the wall. 'How are you going here, Riley? How are you finding camp?'

'It's okay.' I hated the way he kept saying my name.

'Because unlike God I can't be everywhere at once, but I'm hearing things. You had some trouble on the canoe trip. There was an incident this morning – Riley?'

Neville was waiting for an explanation. I had nothing rehearsed, but I felt that if I didn't say something he wouldn't let me leave. 'I just . . . I don't fit in here. Everyone hates me,' I finished lamely.

'Riley. We all have to go through a period of adjustment.'

'Well, I'd rather just go home.'

'Do you want to talk about it?'

I shook my head.

Neville leaned over his desk. 'Look. You're almost at the halfway mark. I'll do you a deal. Just for today, try to participate – I mean *really* participate. If you still feel like this tomorrow – well, we'll call your father and see if we can't sort something out.'

Trevor returned carrying a slide-tray and an overhead projector.

Neville lit up at the sight of him. 'Anyway, you don't want to miss Trevor's talk. The domestic life of the malleefowl is a revelation.'

Trevor grinned. Neville grinned. I understood I was being dismissed. I walked out, and just as I was about to hit the rain again I remembered about Dad being away. I went back to remind Neville. I paused outside his door. It was slightly ajar. I stepped silently across and peeked inside.

Neville was sitting behind his desk and Trevor was leaning over, pointing to some paper or other. I could see them grinning, chuckling. It was a warm sound that made me feel lonely. I suddenly realised I was seeing something private. Neville leaned across and kissed Trevor, *really* kissed him. I backed away from the door, feeling like there was a whole lot of stuff going on that I just couldn't see. Bird had told me when we sat in the dark on the round-about that owls are special because they're the only birds with eyes that face front; I was like all the other birds who can only see out the sides. I wondered what else I had missed.

Why couldn't I call Chloe? I had so much to tell her. We'd sit by her pool in our under-sized bikinis and over-sized sunnies and I'd relay the whole Greek tragedy of infidelity and betrayal and secrets but then I remembered – this was Chloe – scandal was her stock in trade, she wouldn't bat an eyelid. Now, if I told *Sarita* her eyes would bug out and her mouth would pop. She'd get that mad giggle going. She'd look at me with awe. It occurred to me that I didn't want to leave with Sarita hating me. I vowed to spend the remainder of the day getting her back in my pocket.

A Basically Hostile Environment

I entered the rec room for Trevor's talk fully prepared to participate but when I plonked down amongst the Honey-eaters, the hate was evident. Sarita, Fleur, even the twins reacted like those weighted children's toys that start off leaning towards you and then swing wildly in the opposite direction. Soon there was enough space around me for a head-spin or an epileptic seizure. So I spread out. I crossed my legs swami-style, and leaned back on my palms. I lifted my chin and smiled zenly. Only faithful Bird was being nice to me. He scuttled over with a piece of paper

'I need you to do something for me.'

'What?' I looked down at the paper. 'What's this?'

'A request list. Dylan is going into town this afternoon.'

'Okay,' I said. 'What do you need me for?'

'I need you to ask for spark plugs.'

'Why don't you ask for them?'

'Please, Riley. *Please*.'

He looked so pained I almost laughed.

'I love it when you beg.'

I found Dylan. He grunted a greeting.

'Heard you're going into town,' I waved the page at him.

Dylan's eyes were bleary. 'I have to get a new prescription.'

I raised my eyebrows, remembering his portable pharmacy.

'Trevor, "Parks and Wildlife" is giving me a lift after lunch.' He shrugged. 'Just don't ask me to get you anything illegal or period-related.'

'You wouldn't buy me tampons? That's cold.'

I looked at the sheet of paper.

Fleur: Menthol throat lozenges, Evian atomiser. One blue rose.

'Is this a request list or a scavenger hunt?'

Dylan shrugged again.

Laura & Lisa: Violet Crumbles x 2, Family size block of Cadbury Dairy Milk. 2 litre Pepsi Max.

Richard: The Financial Review. Time magazine.

Ethan: sour snakes

Sarita hadn't written anything. I looked at her plaits, her bushy eyebrows. I unclipped the pen and wrote:

Riley: metal comb, sharp scissors, Hella Hot Oil hair conditioner, tweezers.

I could feel Bird staring at my back. I turned to see his panicked grin. He was giving me the thumbs up, clenching his fists so hard I worried he might cut off his own circulation. That can happen. I turned back and wrote, *spark plugs. Don't ask.*

I passed the list to Dylan and turned my attention to

the stage. Trevor and Neville were bonding over the slide projector. They were talking closely. Could they make it any more obvious?

Neville introduced Trevor in exactly the same words that he'd used in his office. Trevor did his broad Aussie 'G'day' and the audience echoed him, ruffling with laughter. Roslyn killed the lights and the first slide came up.

Trevor said, 'This picture is what it's all about. For a while there it looked like we were going to lose the Little Desert. Developers wanted it for farming – if there hadn't been such a massive public outcry, well, we wouldn't be here now. It just goes to show you that sometimes the people have the right idea and sometimes the people actually win.'

Trevor clicked to the next slide. 'This aerial view was taken in the winter. Those ridges there are sand dunes. You see those waterholes – soaks we call them – some of them are recurring salt lakes. Fraser – the bloke who used to own this place before Neville's mob took over – believed that one of the lakes had healing properties.' Trevor looked down and smiled. 'He went a bit loopy-loo in the end. He thought the crater on the south-west of the property was caused by a spaceship – '

Neville coughed loudly. Trevor glanced back at him. 'Righto.' He clicked onto the next slide. 'What are we looking at?'

We all stared. A few dim 'nothings' surfaced. Bird piped up, 'Malleefowl. *Leipoa ocellata*.'

Trevor pointed to a bird camouflaged in the scrub. Echoes of recognition bounced around the room.

'Right. That fella is a lowan bird, aka malleefowl. He's indigenous to the area – but you already knew that, didn't you?'

The Mallees chortled and goggled at their namesake.

'He's a stately gent, I reckon.' Trevor went on. 'You wouldn't know it to look at him but he's just put in a twenty-four-hour day.'

More slides followed the mallee through his workday. Trevor provided the soundtrack. 'The malleefowl is a megapode. That means he doesn't have a typical nest – he's a mound-building bird. Megapodes are rare enough, but the malleefowl is rarer still because they have to incubate their eggs in a basically hostile environment. Think about the extremes in weather you've had just in the last couple of days. This land is a contradiction. It's a desert but it's full of life. And all the flora and fauna here are built to survive. Nature adapts.'

Neville coughed again. Trevor looked across. He readjusted the slides before continuing with a small smile.

'In the mornings the male mallee opens the mound to get the sun in and at night he covers it up against the chill. Throughout the day he fills it with leaves and bark and dead vegetation.'

Bird called out, 'The mounds are a metre deep, I've seen them.'

Trevor smiled. 'Mate. If you could bottle that bird's dedication . . .'

Fleur put her hand up. 'Where's the female mallee bird while all this is happening?'

Trevor laughed, 'Shopping!' Everyone laughed with him. And because I was 'participating' I laughed too, but it sounded hollow and at one point, while my mouth was open and my eyes were desperate, I caught Dylan watching. I longed for a mallee mound big enough to hide in.

On the way out I put my hand on the back of Dylan's chair. 'So what happened to your stash?'

'Someone nicked them.'

'You serious?'

He nodded and made to move off. I kept my hand firm and my head wistful. I wanted to feel close to him. I had a feeling that I could tell him anything and he wouldn't judge me. Dylan turned around and stared at my fingers. 'More wheelchair theory: the chair becomes an extension of the body. A less relaxed Mutard might think you were trying to invade his personal space.'

'Oh.' I tapped my rings against the metal and then fluttered my fingers up and away.

GOD'S GREAT HEARTH

Because of the rain, all outdoor activities were cancelled. The Mallees and Bronzewings got the rec room while the Honeyeaters were sequestered to a steaming portable behind the counsellors' annexe. I sat in the back with my bunker book. It was just past midday – only ten hours until my great escape. Would I make it? I decided my participation would be a kind of social experiment. All the more to entertain Chloe with when I got back. Meanwhile, Roslyn was passing around a box of 'memory crosses'. She stood at the front of the room, cardboard cross in hand, looking like she was about to pop.

'Everyone listen – these are Ter-rif-ic. They're interactive. What you do is . . . you fold the panels over . . . and each time you "switch" you get a different scripture. The pastor who invented these was trying to find a way to help his children memorise scriptures – I heard he started with a paper plane but you can guess what happened there.' Roslyn shook her head as if to say, 'crazy kids' and then she performed this fast switching technique with a madman look in her eye that made me wonder if she hadn't once moonlighted as a croupier.

'See?' Roslyn elicited 'Oohs' with her sleight-of-hand. 'Aren't they nifty? Have a go. It's easy once you get the hang of it. Ter-rif-ic.'

It was easy. The primary school version of the memory cross was the paper fortune teller: Fold a square in fourths, unfold, turn the corners in, then flip and fold again, put your fingers in the slits and switch, switch, switch. In between '*You will be super-famous*' and '*Your crush knows you like him*' there was always poison. '*Everyone knows you pong bad*', '*You will die in a terrible accident*'. Crazy kids.

I held my memory cross aloft. The panels were illustrated with bright colours and dull scriptures and I'd had mine in hand for maybe seven seconds before I let loose with my Sharpie. On the panel that read 'My father's house has many rooms', I changed 'rooms' to 'goons'. I chuckled at my wit and wished I had someone to share it with but even Dylan had taken off his biker gloves and was studiously switching. His hands were smooth and pale and his skin looked tissue-paper thin. I wondered if it were true that the physically impaired developed heightened perception in other senses to compensate for what they'd lost, like how a blind man can hear better. I liked thinking that Dylan's hands were high voltage. I pictured sparks flying as our fingers brushed over his cigarette packet. I wanted to touch his hand, then. I wanted to so much that my mouth went dry.

'Riley?' I nearly jumped. Roslyn was at my shoulder, eyeing off my handiwork. She took the defaced cross out of my hand and sighed. 'You think you're being funny, Riley, but all you're really doing is advertising your ignorance.'

This stung more than it should have. It could have been because she said it so loudly. I asked, 'Why does this make me ignorant?'

She shook her head. 'Godless fools know nothing of scripture.'

The whole idea of Participation went out the window.

'Well, I just can't see how any intelligent person can believe in God,' I declared. 'You can't seriously tell me He's up there watching everybody all of the time. If the Big Man's so powerful, why doesn't He do something about the world going to shit?'

'Let's talk about it,' Roslyn said. 'What does everybody else think?'

Lisa or Laura piped up, 'I think God made man and man made the mess – but if we pray hard enough He will forgive us.'

Roslyn nodded.

'And then what will He do?' I asked.

Lisa/Laura looked at me like the answer was obvious. 'He'll start again, like he did with Noah. He'll take only the best people.'

'Who are the best people?' I demanded to know. 'You?'

'Well, yeah.'

'It says in the Bible – ' Richard started but I stared him down.

'You can't believe in the Bible,' I snapped. 'If you believe in that then you think that women should serve men and that gays have something wrong with them.'

'Yeah!' Craig said. He was grinning. I wanted to slap him.

Ethan whirled around in his chair. 'The scriptures are the word of the Lord. If you don't accept Jesus's teachings then you can't enter the Kingdom of Heaven. You'll suffer in the long run.'

'I'm already suffering.'

Dylan spoke in a low voice. 'You don't know what suffering is.'

Everybody was quiet. I was stunned – I didn't expect to get shit from Dylan. And then I started to get angry. I stumbled over my words. 'You of all people should understand what I'm talking about.'

'Riley,' Roslyn warned.

'What kind of God does that!' I pointed to Dylan's chair.

'Riley, that's quite enough!'

I pressed my forehead on the desk lid. 'I didn't mean . . . forget it.'

Roslyn swayed. 'Let's cool it down, Honeyeaters!' She tried to distract us with more cardboard. 'These are blank memory crosses. I want you to fill these in. You don't have to use His words, you can use your own. Use "positivisms". Write down the nicest thing a person's ever said to you, or the happiest holiday you can remember.'

Dylan put his hand up. 'What if you don't have any . . . posits?'

'Positivisms.' The word had reverb and Roslyn suddenly looked doubtful. I saw what she saw. Apart from the glossy-ad perfection of Fleur and Craig, we were a motley crew. We were the unwanted or unruly, bullies and bed-wetters side by side under God's great hearth.

'Everybody has a positivism,' Roslyn insisted.

Bird burped and then clapped and laughed.

'You reckon?' I muttered.

I opened my blank cross and wrote on the panels:

'Sorry about Craig',

'But seriously, you're not missing much',

'Really',

'We could both do better',

'I have an idea for your new look',

'Let's talk'.

'Smiley face'

'Hugs'

And then I flicked it so that it landed on Sarita's desk. Sarita's hand closed over it. Roslyn swooped down and held out her own hand. Sarita kept hers clenched. Roslyn stared at me. She jerked her palm-tree head and I waited for the coconuts to fall. 'Riley. Outside. Now!'

Bird swung around in his seat. He looked stricken, but I was playing Roslyn's fool, bride-stepping down the aisle, acknowledging each of my 'fellow' Honeyeaters with a neat mechanical nod. Ethan and Richard were glowering at me; Sarita was wide-eyed; Fleur's face was all screwed up, like someone had farted. Craig was smirking. Dylan was leaning back with his arms folded, his eyes as flat as when he'd been handed his token YL vest. I felt myself wilting. I dropped my pose. *What had I done?*

My dressing-down happened outside on the plain in the pouring rain.

Roslyn was 'concerned' for me. She said she understood from Neville that I'd lost my mother and that I was having difficulty 'adjusting'.

'You don't have to tell me being young is difficult – I used to be young,' Roslyn said earnestly. I snorted.

'It's the time when you most often feel like you can't talk to anyone, but truly, Riley, talking is the best thing for you. If you don't want to talk to me then talk to God. That's what He's here for. Outside you're laughing but inside you're screaming, right?'

Right.

Roslyn made soothing sounds. 'Riley, I feel your pain. Look at you – you're like *this* – ' she made an impression of a loon in a straitjacket. I wanted to claw at her crow's feet and spit on her halo.

She rubbed my shoulder. 'You're all closed up. What are you thinking? Just say it.'

So I said it. Or rather I started saying it but ended up shouting it.

'I don't believe in you, Roslyn. I don't believe in Spirit Ranch. And I don't believe in your God. He let my mother die a week before I got my first period when I really could have used the girl-talk. He gave me a wonky cycle. Which in turn made the doctor put me on the pill. Which in turn made me fat. Which in turn made me anxious.'

Roslyn had her hands on my shoulders but I could not stop.

'So then I'm fourteen and on the pill and do you think HE stops the rumour mill? NO. So boys are starting to notice me – great – until AFTER when said boys bark at me like I'm a dog. HE could have done something about that. Don't you think?'

Roslyn's mouth was open. She winced and twitched and her eyes looked like lines, just lines jumping around a page.

'And just when things are starting to get normal and I have a friend who does mad stuff and I have a guy who likes me, HE sends me here. So you tell me, Roslyn, because I can't see, I just can't see what HIS divine plan is unless it's to drive me completely fucking crazy.'

Somebody clapped. Someone else giggled. I looked up. Every single window of the portable had a face in it. All of the Honeyeaters knew my pain. I had laid myself open but Roslyn was wrong on that score too because I didn't feel better, I felt a hundred times worse.

Assorted Guys

The sun was back out on this most schizophrenic of days. I skipped lunch and the off-site activity and went back to Fraser's house, where I smoked and read *Utopia* and schemed a running order for my great escape. Dinner would be finishing around seven, and then there'd be campfire jollies. Dylan would have returned by then, so I could pack up Sarita's make-over kit, with instructions, and she'd still get to be beautiful and maybe forgive me. There was going to be a movie later. That gave me just over an hour to walk to Nhill. Thank God I'd brought my combat boots.

But time seemed to stop at Fraser's house. I couldn't hear anything except birds. And the excitement I was feeling about my future escape kept bumping up against worry. What if the night never came and all I had was this day – this series of humiliations? What if what happened at camp *didn't* stay at camp?

I ground my cigarette into the sand and sent myself on a lazy spin on the roundabout. Craig's face, blank and bastardly, circled my mind. I pushed it away and tried to concentrate on my imminent freedom, but his face came back laughing. More faces came – assorted guys from adventures past – Noah 'Krakatoa' and Murray from the milk bar – tumbles all the way down the conveyer belt to Aaron Becker. All those guys and they all had the same expression, because none of them *really* liked me. And I didn't *really* like them. I just liked to feel liked. I knew all this. I wasn't stupid. I also knew that just because I could get a guy off didn't mean I was skilled. 'It's not rocket science, Riley,' Chloe had said. 'It's friction.'

Now I was having a horrible memory flash. Once – pretty soon after we moved – I hooked up with a guy whose girlfriend was in my class. She was Fleur-ish – one of those beautiful bitches – so I didn't feel bad about betraying her. But after the deed (school dance, emergency exit stairwell) I turned up to school to see my locker plastered with stickers that said fatgirlsaregrateful.com. And I tried to be subtle about taking them off but they were cheap stickers, they threaded weirdly, they got all in my nails and left a sticky mess. But I guess I should have been used to that.

'Hey Riley?' Bird was standing at the top of the garage stairs. 'Do you want to see something?'

I pretended not to hear him and he went back inside with his shoulders slumped. But curiosity got the better of me. When I peered around the garage door I saw that the tarp was off the VW. And the VW was off the blocks. It had tyres now – great big fat ones. Bird was sitting in the driver's seat flicking the indicators. When he saw me he stood and wiped his hands too many times on his jeans. I opened the door of the passenger side and got in. We were high up. I bounced in the seat. 'Nice ride.'

'It's a dune buggy. She was born a 1967 VW Beetle. We had to cut her chassis.' Bird looked apologetic.

'We who?'

Bird shook his head. 'Fraser and me. I'm just finishing her off.'

'Is this one of your "special duties"?'

'No. No one knows about this. Just you and my sister.' Bird's face became fraught. 'You won't tell, will you?'

'Of course not.' I crossed myself for good measure. 'Why are the tyres so fat?'

'They're sand tyres. When she's ready she'll practically be able to go vertical.' Bird kept saying 'she' with an air of protectiveness that was sweet.

'Does *she* have a name?' I asked.

He flushed and looked away. I heard him mumble, 'Not yet.'

'Does *she* go?'

Bird smiled. 'Almost.'

'Right, spark plugs.'

Bird nodded. 'Dylan will be in town by now.'

I sighed and leaned back in the seat. 'I wish she went. I'd take her.'

'Can you drive?' Bird asked.

'Almost.'

'Riley?'

'What?'

'I like you.'

He was staring at the windscreen and blushing furiously. His hands gripped the wheel. 'When you said that to Roslyn . . . about a guy who likes you. Well, I do too.'

'Aww, sweet.' I patted his hand. 'Thanks, Bird.'

'I've never met anyone like you,' he said.

I looked at him. I had a sudden image of the male malleefowl, tending its nest 24/7. That was devotion. I kissed Bird on the cheek lightly and he held his breath. 'Don't hyperventilate.'

SHE'S SO SATAN

And the rain hammered down . . .

In cabin three I lay on my bed and stared at the wash, and wondered if it would ever stop. I didn't want to make my great escape under flood conditions. What if I fell in a soak? Or some quicksand? Trevor said the desert was full of holes. Craig wasn't going to abseil to save *me*. When Sarita and Fleur came in I pretended I was sleeping.

'Look at that,' Fleur said. 'I haven't been able to eat since she came.'

'You never eat.'

'That's not true,' Fleur insisted. 'I had lunch. Shut up.' She sighed heavily. 'Where's Dylan and my lozenges?'

'Fleur, I have to go and perform my ablutions now,' Sarita said.

'Do you know how gross that sounds?'

I heard a thump. Fleur cried out, 'That bitch! Look what she's drawn on my bed. She's *so* Satan. I'm going to tell Neville.'

'Don't.'

'Sarita – why are you sticking up for her?' Fleur sniffed.

'Please, Fleur. I have a headache.'

'You should lie down with a wet cloth on your head. I'll get you one.'

Fleur left. The bunk creaked as Sarita climbed up the ladder.

I heard her unfolding some paper, over and over. I peeked out from under my hair. She was sitting on the end of her bed with the memory cross I'd written for her, switching the panels and reading my words again and again and again.

Fond Farewell

I was on my way to the mess hall for dinner when I saw Trevor's ute pull into the parking lot. I lingered by the wall, waiting for Dylan. But he didn't show. There was only Trevor, headed for Neville's office with his hat in his hand and a frown. Where was Dylan?

There were some edgy heads at the Honeyeaters' table. They wanted their goodies.

'Dylan's got our money,' Ethan said darkly.

Richard shook his head. 'He's probably halfway to Queensland.'

I rolled my eyes. 'Because it'd be so easy to hitchhike in a wheelchair.'

'Sympathy,' Richard sniffed.

'Retard,' I returned.

Fleur gave a pathetic cough, and shuddered like she was on her deathbed. I tried to catch Sarita's eye but she was still ignoring me. How many times did I have to say I was sorry? Maybe the memory cross wasn't enough. Maybe she wanted me to write it in the sky. Where was Dylan? Sarita would never get her (hair) care package now. She'd never know how close she came to looking good. And as for me, my watch was set, my bag was packed, my Goth Lolita dress was hanging up to dry. The only thing standing between me and freedom was Time.

Post-dinner, the Honeyeaters gathered by the barbeque for campfire jollies. The sun had started its slow descent. Craig had his guitar out. He was singing and to look at him you'd never believe he was anything but honest. He sang a few Jesus-y numbers before moving on to an old song, a Dadrock standard about life and cycles and mortality. Fleur joined in with her anorexic pitch. She cupped one ear and swayed from side to side. It was all so uncool – it should have been funny, but I found myself feeling a prickle of sadness. Minor chords can do that. It occurred to me that I might miss people: Olive, Bird, Sarita. I didn't want to think about Dylan, because when I did I felt stupid and full of *should've*.

And then it was nine o'clock and everything was going to plan. The movie was *Pay It Forward*. I sat through half an hour, with one eye on my watch. Just after the little kid introduces his wild idea (when someone does you a favour, don't pay it back, pay it forward) I left my seat and tiptoed up to Roslyn's chair.

'I have a headache,' I whispered. 'May I be excused?'

Roslyn was engrossed. She waved me away and I walked out the door and didn't look back.

*

In cabin three I turned the light on and stopped with a start. I had thought Sarita was in the rec room along with everyone else – but there was her arm hanging down from the bunk. She was asleep. I studied her face; it looked peaceful, dreamy. I was toying with the idea of waking her to say goodbye. I wondered again about Dylan, and if Sarita would know what to do with the Hella Hot Oil, or if Bird would ever get his spark plugs. My mind jumped from thought to thought, face to face until I felt dizzy and had to sit down. This was real. I was *really* going. But the flipside of excitement was tension. I was getting the nervous sweats. I checked myself. *Riley*, I told myself. *Breathe. Think. Get your suitcase. Fuck the fond farewells; no one will miss you when you are gone.*

I stuffed my suitcase with clothes and jewels and war paint and snapped the locks shut. I checked my watch again. Fifteen minutes had passed in a second. I had to *move*! I paused at the door holding Roslyn's shroud like the white hanky of surrender. Then I hopped up on Fleur's bed and draped the shroud across Sarita's chest. A puff of air escaped her lips. I heard something scatter and looked down to see little white pills everywhere. Sarita moaned and rolled slightly to the left. I saw something white under her waist. I reached for it. It was Dylan's missing vial – *after four, it depends on your tolerance*, he'd said. But I had no way of knowing how many Sarita had taken.

My first thought was not of my escape, or of time escaping – that came later. I prodded Sarita. I called her name. She didn't move. 'Oh Shit.' Her eyes remained closed.

I threw my suitcase down. 'Okay, keep breathing. I'll get help.'

I opened the door to Fleur. She scowled automatically. I pulled her inside. When she saw the look of panic on my face she sucked back her barbs. 'What?'

'Sarita took Dylan's pills. I don't know how many.'

Fleur looked up. She started climbing the bunk bed ladder.

'I'm going to get Neville,' I told her.

'Wait.' Fleur put her index finger to her mouth and bit off her nail. She dragged Sarita into a sitting position. Sarita's eyes popped open. Her mouth started to go, 'Wha – ?' but then Fleur stuck her finger in it. I could see Sarita's eyes racing. She was trying to protest, but then she heaved and liquid flooded from her mouth. It got in Fleur's hair, but Fleur didn't even flinch. She turned to me. 'Never fails.' She poked her finger in Sarita's mouth again. This time Sarita's teeth clamped down on it. 'Ow!' Fleur yanked her finger out and wiped it on the bedspread. 'Ingrate.'

'Fleur!' Sarita managed to splutter. '*What are you doing?*'

I answered for her. 'What are *you* doing?' I threw the vial at her. 'Are you crazy? Taking pills . . . do you have any idea how *fucked* that is?' My heart was beating super-fast and my hands were trembling.

Sarita's face went redder and redder. Then she burst out with: 'But I was only pretending!'

'*What?*'

'Really. I was being a drama queen.' Sarita coughed gingerly. She stuck her tongue out and winced.

'I thought you'd OD'd,' I said, dazedly.

Fleur started laughing. 'That's twisted!'

I looked at Sarita. She was biting her lip trying to suppress a smile. 'I thought it would be funny.'

'There's nothing funny about death,' I said.

'Riley, Riley,' Sarita echoed my earlier advice. 'You have to lighten up.'

Relief and anger snuck up on me. It filled all the hollow places inside me. It felt like a sugar high. And then, somehow, I was laughing. It *was* twisted, but it was funny. Who knew Sarita could do funny? After she'd wiped the tears from her eyes, Sarita mocked herself, 'Always someone is saving me . . . ' Her lips formed a straight line. 'And now I must go and perform my ablutions.'

Fleur groaned. 'You do that.'

After Sarita left we laughed again. We smiled goofily for a few seconds before returning to form. Fleur eyed my suitcase. 'Going somewhere?'

I looked at my watch. 'Shit!'

WALKABOUT

I ran. Past the plain, past the toilets, past Fraser's house where the light was on and Bird was tinkering, making a kind of night music. I ran past the walled garden and the evil roundabout, along the path now thinned to a strip, sandwiched by scrub. I felt brave, lawless and wild. With each slap of boot on sand, hope hammered in my heart. But hope is just a four-letter word. I was starting to worry. I should have hit bitumen by now. Then I tripped and fell. That was the only way I was going to stop. Then I knelt in the dirt and shouted in frustration and exhaustion. I'd screwed up. I'd underestimated the distance between camp and the road. It was 10.28 and I was too late. Going forward was pointless but going back was worse. I pressed on.

By the time I reached the road to Nhill, I had a stitch and my breath was staggered. As I walked I tried to make a rational plan: I would find a phone booth, I would call Chloe and appeal to her sense of adventure. Never mind that it was a five-hour drive from Melbourne and Chloe didn't have a car. I closed by eyes and took a deep breath.

Walking, walking. Hup Two. Now that I had a new plan I concentrated on my surroundings. The night was big and beautiful and *mine*. I was looking up at a huge cathedral ceiling with no clear end. And under it Neville's rave about smallness and bigness didn't seem so stupid. I was power-walking now. It was weird, because even dead-tired I could feel exhilaration bubbling up. Was this because of exercise? Endorphins? I thought of Dad, post spin class sporting a Rorschach of sweat on the back of track-pants, red-faced and singing Gilbert & Sullivan. Maybe Norma had something.

In a parallel universe I was on the bus. I was pressing my face to the window and watching the scenery fade to black. In another parallel universe I had slipped out of the swimming pool five minutes before the cops turned up and Ben Seb and I were solid – we walked with our hands in each other's back pockets and swapped spit under streetlights. In another parallel universe my mum was making a dress for me out of silver voile, and I was holding my breath against probable pin-jabs. 'Don't move,' she warned me. 'Don't even breathe.' When she was finished I didn't even recognise myself. I was her creation. I slinked and shimmered like water under the sun.

I almost wanted Roslyn to appear so I could ask her if a parallel universe discounted God. What kind of God was there for a girl like me? Why couldn't I just choose a God, like I'd choose a pair of shoes? *Me and* Utopia*'s Thomas More*, I thought, *we'll give you gods*. And then I giggled. I'd been infected. My next step was snake-handling and speaking in tongues. I had to find a phone booth.

Nhill looked like a sketch from an Australian history textbook. All tin roofs and lacework, screen doors, and sleepy verandas. I stood in the middle of the road and wavered. I couldn't see a phone booth. I couldn't see any lights on anywhere. As I stood in the empty silence, a wave of hopelessness came over me. I didn't want to walk anymore. I was *tired*. Maybe I'd find a pub or a church or a police station or a psycho killer. But what was I *really* looking for? I sat on the curb and stared at a grain silo in the distance and tried to empty my head of all thoughts.

A utility pulled up. Inside was Trevor, 'Parks and Wildlife'. Slumped in the passenger seat was a very drunk Dylan Luck.

Trevor had his elbow out the window. 'You gone walkabout?'

I shrugged. I felt weird, leaden. I was angry with myself, the whole disaster, but I was also feeling this massive relief that I didn't have to walk anymore.

Trevor jerked his head. 'Get in.'

I opened the passenger door. Dylan looked cute, all floppy and irresponsible. He shook himself alert and inched over to the middle seat. He smiled at me sheepishly. 'What are you doing here?'

'What are *you* doing here?'

Trevor lowered the handbrake. 'There's one every year.'

He rolled back onto the highway. I wound the window all the way down – to match my face. The air gave me cool kisses and whispered of the things I couldn't have – like Freedom, Escape and Ben Sebatini. Dylan leaned into my shoulder and pressed his face against my skin. He nuzzled my arm. I thought about shrugging him off, but I let it ride . . . it felt nice, comforting, so after a while I just let him. When he put his hand on my thigh I didn't do anything about that either. He kept it there all the way back to camp.

Neville was waiting outside his office when Trevor dropped us off. He was wearing a brown-and-purple terry-towelling robe and his bald spot shone in the moonlight. Trevor got Dylan's chair out of the back and snapped it expertly into place. He helped Dylan into it and then tipped his hat to Neville. 'Do you want me to stick around?'

Neville squeezed Trevor's shoulder. He looked so tired and over it. He was trapped in his role as good counsellor as much as I was trapped in mine as camp renegade. Neville sighed. He spread his arms as if he might gather us up. 'Let's go.'

Inside his office Neville fixed himself some coffee. He sat in his chair and sipped it and stared at us. No one said anything for a long time. Finally Neville put his cup down. 'Okay. What have you got to say for yourselves?'

'Sorry, chief,' Dylan slurred. I didn't say anything.

'I've been running this camp for fifteen years,' Neville told us. 'There's nothing I haven't seen.' His tough-guy stance only lasted a few seconds, then he crumpled. He cradled his face and wiped his eyes and spoke as if to himself. 'How have I failed you? How can I help you?'

'We were trying to help ourselves,' I muttered. If Dylan minded me speaking for him he didn't say anything. Not that he was capable of saying much in his inebriated state. His eyes opened and he smiled fuzzily.

'Are you going to send us home now?' I was smiling too. I saw Chloe shaking her head and saying, '*My friend, my friend, you've got him.*' Dylan and I had been wildly disobedient – how could Neville let us stay? Expulsion was just as good as escape – it was all a means to an end.

Neville thought about my question. He drummed his fingers on the desk. 'No, Riley. Sending you home would only make all of us look bad. And what would you have learnt?' He stood up and flexed like a man of action. 'Go to your cabin, Riley. I'll take Dylan to his. I'll work out what to do with you both in the morning.'

ON THE FOURTH DAY

NEVERMORE

Squeaalllll. Clank. 'Attention campers. This is your thought for the day: *He that hath findeth his life shall lose it, and he that loseth his life for my sake shall find it.*' Squeeallll. Clank.

Fleur stretched and yawned and said to no one in particular, 'That makes absolutely no sense.' Her eyes flicked over me. 'Are you *still* here?'

I checked under the covers. 'I think so.'

She gave me a smile that was all lip. She eyed the bottom of Sarita's bunk and knocked on the slats. 'Hey! Are you alive?'

Sarita was lying on her side with her eyes open, staring, thinking. She reminded me of this painting by Paul Gauguin called *Nevermore*. I used to see it every day on the back of the toilet door. Mum had bought the print at the Guggenheim in a mid-twenties New York meltdown moment. There was a story to it, she said. The girl in the picture was afraid of death and so she would not close her eyes to sleep. Gauguin was a French Impressionist/escape artist. He ran away to Tahiti to paint Island girls in various states of undress. Sarita looked just like one of his waking beauties, with her hair out and her staring eyes – except of course she was wearing her neck-to-knee nightie. Suddenly I realised I didn't know where that print was. It hadn't come with us to the new house.

I rolled out of bed and hunched over the mirror. Last night's make-up had gone South. I took my eye make-up off and then re-applied my lipstick, slowly, methodically.

'Take it easy with that thing,' Fleur advised.

I stuck my tongue out at her, and looked at my reflection. Gaudy me. The lipstick *was* too much. And it was too early in the morning.

Sarita swung her feet over the bunk and announced, 'Today is the first day of the rest of my life.' She said it as though she really *had* tried to commit suicide.

'My life is over,' I murmured. I was thinking about *Nevermore* and about my mother and how she wasn't scared and she'd closed her eyes. Then I remembered where I was, and my admission felt like a slip. The concerned glances from Fleur and Sarita sent me rushing to protect myself. I camped it up. 'My life left on the 10.30 bus.' I waved my hands around my body. 'This that you see is but a hollow shell.'

Fleur groaned. 'You two should be onstage.'

Sarita whispered, 'Yes.' She held up her prayer rock and kissed it, then she tossed Roslyn's shroud at me. 'Here – you need this.'

'Ta.' I blotted my lipstick on the shroud and wedged it in the corner of the mirror. Sarita opened her mouth and closed it, then opened it again. 'Today is the first day of the rest of my life,' she repeated.

I threw my pillow at her. 'Stop saying that!'

The three of us made sleepy steps towards the shower block. Anyone watching us would have thought that we were great friends. We stood languidly in the queue. We were less guarded than on other mornings, and chatted amiably, spontaneously, about nothing. Someone had forgotten her toothbrush. Someone else had forgotten to flush. The steam rose up from the showers and carried with it the scent of peach shampoo. The hot water supply was on the spaz. Someone kept dropping the soap. We shook water from our ears, and put dry clothes on over wet legs. We raked our tangles with our fingers and when Roslyn blew the breakfast bugle we dashed across the plain. The order of the day was same-same, but for some reason everything felt different.

At breakfast the Honeyeaters were buzzing. Dylan scattered his town booty across the table. Bird cast me a meaningful look and patted one of his vest pockets. Fleur popped a lozenge. She pinched her throat and allowed a fruity 'Me, may, ma, mo, mooo' into the fug. The twins dismissed their All-Bran and ripped into the chocolate. They passed the bar around. I hesitated when it came to me. I was waiting for Fleur to say something snide about comfort eating but she was warbling away, oblivious. I took a piece. Dylan passed me a paper shopping bag. 'This is yours.'

Inside it were the tools that would transform Sarita, spark plugs and something else – a bamboo-covered book.

'What's this for?' I opened the notebook. The first few pages had rough sketches of flowers on them. I looked from the pictures to Dylan.

'It's not – ' he started to say, then threw up his hands. 'It's just a book.'

'Um. Thanks.' The night before came back to me. Dylan's hand on my thigh.

Sarita banged her cup on the table with a force that surprised us all. 'Honeyeaters. I must have your attention.' She was sitting stiffly with her clipboard propped in front of her. 'Honeyeaters. I am floor-managing the talent show. Thus far we have only two entrants. This is dire. I want to know: what are we going to do about it?'

'Sarita!' I grinned. 'You're so *forceful*!' Something had unleashed her big balls sleep-talking voice. I liked it.

Sarita went pink. 'Roslyn has agreed to let us spend The Word planning the shebang.' She checked her clipboard. 'Craig and Fleur are singing, and Lisa and Laura are performing a liturgical dance. Who else?'

Bird put his hand up. 'I could do birdcalls again.'

Ethan and Richard groaned.

'Brilliant.' Sarita wrote his name down.

'I could do a striptease,' I suggested.

There was a moment of silence and then the table erupted into laughter. Even Ethan and Richard joined in.

And then I was laughing too. I felt high and . . . unified. I didn't have my bunker book with me. I wasn't scoffing. I was *participating*.

'Oh my Goodness!' Sarita spluttered. 'I don't think that would go down very well with the parents.'

'It was a joke, Sarita.'

Dad and Norma. As far as they knew I was abseiling and canoeing and group-hugging and cultivating a hot chocolate/*He is Lord* habit. I tried to scowl. I wanted to keep my anti in check but a smile kept creeping back.

Craig moseyed over during the last wave of mirth.

'What's so funny?' he wanted to know.

Dylan looked at me. 'You had to be there.'

Fleur quickly put her bitch back in gear. 'Hey Riley,' she called out. 'Do you want my roll?' She sent her plate spinning towards me.

Richard's face lit up. 'Have mine too, Riley.' He pushed his plate forward.

'Go on, girl's gotta eat.' Ethan mirrored his friend's move. I had bread coming at me from all quarters. I was unprepared for this attack, but I hadn't reckoned on Sarita. She lunged forward and emptied her fruit salad over Fleur's head. Fleur's face – what we could see of it – went white. She peeled a fried egg off her plate and flung it at Sarita who managed to duck just in time. The egg landed on Roslyn's palm-tree head sunny-side down. I heard gasps and laughter and then the room fell silent as if catching its breath. Moments later a random Bronzewing kicked back his chair and hollered, 'Food fight!' and then the sky above the mess hall was thick with buttered buns and bacon shrapnel.

Sarita and I used our trays as shields. We ran blindly through the battlefield, shrieking all the way. Outside we collapsed on the spidergrass.

'Sarita, that was beautiful.' I gripped my stomach. My sides hurt, my face hurt, *everything* hurt but it also felt mad wild good. Sarita sat up. She bubbled with pride. 'There is always a food fight at camp. But this is the first time I have been an instigator.'

I laughed. Sarita had fried-egg sideburns and the ink of delirium in her eyes. She said, 'Something is happening, Riley. I'm going tropical.'

'I think you mean troppo.' I put my hand on her forehead. 'You're crazy from the heat. You'd better lie down.'

Sarita lay back down, spread her arms and made snow angels in the grass.

Involved

The Honeyeaters had to clean up the mess hall. I'd just picked up a sponge when I heard my name over the PA. *'Riley Rose and Dylan Luck, please report to Neville outside the rec room.'* I never liked my name until I heard it next to his. Riley and Dylan, Dylan and Riley. Our Y's and L's had a pleasing assonance. Dylan winked. I threw down my sponge. 'I can't believe we don't get to clean!'

Neville was wearing a smug smile and a green mohair cardigan. This morning's badge said: *Holy Roller.* We saluted him and he stamped his heels together. 'This way.'

We headed to Fraser's house. He stopped at the recycle cage to grab some flattened-out cardboard boxes. He loaded us up and spooled Dylan's arm with two rolls of packing tape. He paused at the door, dangling a bunch of keys. 'Come see the paradise.'

Fraser was more than a packrat. He was a crazy-man hoarder. Every inch of his three-roomed cottage was covered with cans, food packaging, fliers, newspapers, clothes and curiosities like spindles and specimen bottles and eight-track cartridges. Neville carved a path for Dylan. He started assembling the boxes, tearing off tape with his teeth. After he'd exhausted his He-man antics he cleared his throat. 'Riley, Dylan. Your task is to get this house in order. These boxes are for clothes. These boxes are for books. These boxes are for nick-nacks. Any papers can go in the recycling, and general rubbish can go in those bin bags. Questions?'

'What do you classify as a nick-nack?' Dylan queried.

Neville sighed. He picked up an ancient Matchbox car and slapped it in Dylan's palm. 'Use your discretion.'

'Where's it all going to go?' I asked.

'Charity.' Neville looked around at the mess almost belligerently. 'Fraser didn't have any family. He had a kelpie, but the dog went mad around the same time he did.'

'It was the desert,' I whispered melodramatically.

Dylan went, 'Shhhhh!'

We shivered at the possible presence of ghosts.

'But Neville – ' I whined. 'We're going to miss The Word. I was really looking forward to helping plan the talent show.'

'You were going to get involved, were you?'

I smiled bright and fake. Dylan guffawed.

Neville turned to him. 'You too, huh?'

Dylan blanched.

'Gotcha!' Neville's grin only lasted a second. 'Now, get to work,' he growled. 'And see what you can do about this dust.' He stabbed the air with a newly blackened finger and stalked out the door.

'Well,' Dylan said. 'I suppose we should work on our dance routine.'

It was his defeatist voice that made me flare up. Was it so ludicrous to think that he might be able to do something, anything?

'Nice. FYI People in wheelchairs *can* dance. I saw a show in the city once. For school.'

Dylan tutted and looked away.

'Actually it was good,' I went on. 'It was called Dance with a Difference. The dancers were all in wheelchairs but not all of them were . . . you know . . . *disabled*.'

'Hate that word,' Dylan muttered.

'The audience didn't know who was or who wasn't and in the end it didn't even matter.'

Sky – the patchouli lit teacher – had taken the class as part of a workshop on 'expression'. Afterwards she was all, '*Who* has the handicap? Ask yourself that.'

I considered telling Dylan this, but when I looked at him he was busy vogueing, Madonna-style. His face was frozen in an exaggerated wink. Now he had a finger in his dimple and a coy glint in his eye. Now he'd seen the face of death, and was spooked to all eternity. With each 'look' he used his hands to frame his face appropriately. It was his 'startled indignation' complete with fingertips on nipples that got me giggling.

'You should do that for the talent show.'

'I should rise from the chair and do Cossack dancing,' Dylan countered. He folded his arms and nodded like a demented Russian.

'Hmm.' I tried to be serious but the image was too funny, and even Dylan couldn't keep his scowl straight.

THE STORY OF FEBRUARY 2

Fraser's books were old and battered and really, really read. Some had leather covers and gilt lettering; others were barely bound. They were mostly science, religion and natural history. I gasped when I saw the same copy of *Utopia* as the one Chloe had given me.

'What?' Dylan spoke around his cigarette.

I held it up. 'I have this book.'

'Oh yeah, I've seen you reading it. What is it?'

'It's good. You should read it.' I tossed the book. Dylan ducked and *Utopia* landed on the dustbowl. He picked it up. 'Always throwing things at me.'

I looked at him. 'Are you even going to help?'

'What can *I* do?'

'Clear out those papers.' I pointed to the desk. 'And nix the fag. This is tinderbox country.'

Dylan was miffed. 'You know, we don't *have* to do this. Neville only put us here because he doesn't know where else to put us.'

'I know.' I pulled down a handful of books and started

stacking. 'But I tried to take the low road and look where it got me. If I don't keep busy I'll go nuts. I never thought it would be so difficult to just *leave*.'

'How hard is it? You've got legs.'

'Ha ha.' I stopped stacking. Something had occurred to me. It was obvious but I wanted to hear it from him. 'Were you trying to leave?'

'I'm *always* trying to leave,' Dylan said.

'Here?' I was confused. I drew a circle in the air to signify Spirit Ranch.

Dylan pointed to his head. 'Here.'

That was when I asked him how it happened.

He smiled for a long while. 'You took your time.'

'Okay.' Dylan started slowly. 'This is the story of February 2. This guy, Brett, invited a few of us up to his parents' farm. We were going to make a no-budget horror movie, then we found the beer. I'd never been drunk before. Really. I had a bit of a thing about it, like *My body is a temple*. But everyone else was . . . doing it . . . so.

'After we started drinking, the night had no order. I can remember lying out in a paddock and everything looked soft. I remember trying to stare out the cows. I fucking hate cows. And then we all had a go on the tractor. I tried to do a donut. Stupid. I remember this noise – like a wave crashing over my head. And the sky and the ground came together. When it stopped rolling there was this silence and then there was just like . . . a flood.' Dylan opened his mouth and I heard white noise, the roar of a footy crowd, the sound of a shell. 'I remember the ambo's breath smelled like bananas and Brett's dog wouldn't stop barking. I thought the reason I couldn't move was because I was stuck under the tractor. But then they got me out and I still couldn't move.' He squinted and shook his head.

I swallowed. 'Wow.'

'Yeah. Wow,' Dylan echoed. 'And just before it happened I saw a shooting star.'

'Really?'

'Nah.' He smiled briefly and counted off. 'Two months in the hospital, then four months in rehab, then back home with ongoing physical therapy. The doctors do this pinprick test – "Can you feel that?" "No." They go higher – "Can you feel that?" With me the pin stopped here.' He sliced his hand into the top of his thigh. 'I'm what you call incomplete. My spinal cord wasn't completely severed, just partially. In Mutard that's a good thing – it leaves you some wiggle room. If you're complete that means there's no going back.'

My words were out before I could stop them. 'Oh, Dylan.'

He gave me a funny look. 'Don't cry for me, Argentina. It was my own dumb fault. I've been living with it for ten months, twelve days and seven hours. I'm almost used to it. Sometimes – usually first thing when I wake up – I forget. I go to get out of bed like I used to, and then I remember and it's like a blind coming down or a slap around the head.' Dylan clapped his hands, and the sound echoed throughout Fraser's house.

MAD PEOPLE

What would you have learnt? Neville had asked me. That first morning at Fraser's house I was getting a different kind of education. I learnt that:

1. Domestic cleaning may result in mirth;
2. Only mad people write things down;
3. Last summer, Dylan touched Fleur's breast (the right one).

Fraser had gone for a horizontal-over-vertical stacking 'system' so it took most of our time to break down the wall of books. Right at the back, there were two shelves of uniform black notebooks. I flicked through one. There were maps and diagrams and equations. Fraser's handwriting was cramped. He was big on underlining and spiral doodles. I passed the notebook to Dylan. He opened it up a crack and then slammed it shut as if it was cursed.

'Have you seen the movie *Seven*?' he asked me.

'I can't watch anything with Brad Pitt in it,' I said. 'He's too smug.'

'He's not smug when he gets his wife's head in a courier box.'

'Mmm.' I wasn't really listening. 'It shits me how everyone's so beautiful in the movies. The whole world wants to pay money to see beautiful people doing bad things. It's sick. Brad Pitt gets paid a fortune just because he has good genes.' I shrugged. 'He collects art. He makes films about people dying in Tibet or wherever and then spends thousands on a painting that some guy made by spraying paint out of his bum.'

Dylan gave me a strange look. 'You know a lot about Brad Pitt.'

'My mum bought those magazines. Used to. Also, I hate the way you never see fat people on the screen unless they're white trash or retarded or a criminal or all of the above. A fat girl on film is either there for laughs or to gross people out. Unless the film's about the fat girl's "journey" to social acceptance through weight loss. Where's the happy fat girl? That's what I want to know. Hmmph.'

'Okay, you hate movies,' Dylan smiled. 'What do you actually like?'

'Huh?' I was supposed to have a pithy 'personals' answer. *I like sunsets and romantic walks on the beach and playing the ukelele.*

I could say I liked trouble. Or whatever Chloe had lined up for the weekend. Actually, I liked reading, but that was my secret – I didn't do it around Chloe. I used to read with Dad, but he hadn't cracked a book since Norma – all they read was the back of food packaging. Then there was drama.

I used to put on mini-plays with Mum. I know she hoped I'd eventually study it, but the future was a long way away and all bets were off. Plus it wasn't cool to be passionate – every geek in the library knows that much. I used to wish it were the Middle Ages so I could run off with the travelling players. Now I just wanted to run. Mum said that words changed when you spoke them out loud. I had no words for Dylan. But he must have known I was feeling sketchy because he didn't press; after a few beats of silence he simply breezed back to *Seven*.

'What I was going to say was that the killer in *Seven* has notebooks just like these, row upon row upon row.' He paused to give me the 'crazy eyes'. 'Only mad people write things down.'

I arched an eyebrow. 'You think we'll find a body in the next room?'

'Maybe.'

We both took a breath and bolted for the door. Dylan won. He blocked me with his chair, and I couldn't get around him. I laughed and laughed – that crazy corpsing kind of laughter that actors get when they can't say a line without convulsing. Eventually I dropped to the floor, and rolled from side to side. 'I'm dying,' I groaned. 'You're killing me.'

Dylan pulled his crutch out and jabbed me lightly in the shoulder.

'Die, you crazy bitch! Die, die hence!'

Are you Rampant?

Eventually I recovered. I sat up and regarded him seriously. 'Why did you get me that notebook when you went to town? Do you think *I'm* mad?'

'Hell yeah!' Dylan laughed.

'How am I mad?'

'Well, most people try to avoid trouble. You go for it with open arms. Also, for someone who wears a lot of black, you're very colourful. You're like this . . . action feature where there's so much going on that the audience can't tell who they're supposed to be barracking for.'

'You think I'm larger than life,' I cracked, puffing my cheeks out like a cane toad. 'Bleugh.'

'I don't mean it like that. It's supposed to be a compliment.'

'Oh.' I was feeling strange flutters in my belly. 'Oh.'

Dylan was staring at me, not smiling. I looked down and rearranged my shirt. He nodded at me in the deliberate-casual manner of a high school drug dealer. 'So who's the guy you were talking about?'

'What guy?' I remembered my rant. 'Oh. Ben.'

'What's Ben like?'

I shrugged. With Chloe I'd talk about Ben to distraction, but suddenly I was having trouble identifying what it was I actually liked about him. Ben was a beautiful face, a challenge. He was doing his electrician's apprenticeship. He was nineteen but still lived with his parents. He put most of his wages into his Monaro. He liked beer and pot. I *thought* he liked me but now I was once removed, I wasn't sure about that either.

Dylan was waiting. I said, 'Ben's follically challenged. He bet his mates he'd grow a totally gay moustache for Movember – the charity thing?'

Dylan looked blank.

'Guys get sponsored to grow moustaches in November. It's this collective Burt Reynolds fetish. Anyway, Ben tried and he couldn't grow one. And now he has this – ' I giggled again, ' – this *tuft*.' I put a finger under my nose. 'Here.' I started laughing. 'And he won't shave it off.'

When Dylan was just about to smile his eyes went first, and his face seemed to lift and lighten. His mouth wiggled. 'A tuft?'

'A tuft.'

Dylan and I laughed about the tuft even more than we'd laughed about the body. It was like Fraser's house ran on nitrous oxide. If ever the wave of hilarity died down, one of us would bleat 'Tuft!' and the laughter would start all over again. I put my head between my legs and remembered to breathe. When I finally looked up Dylan was leaning back in his chair, smiling lazily down at me. A lock of hair kept falling across his eye, and I pictured myself crawling over to him, placing my hands on his knees, putting my face close to his and softly blowing. Where had *that* come from? My blood sugar levels must have been dipping.

'I touched Fleur's breast once,' Dylan confessed. 'The right one. We were doing a Trust exercise where you have to sit opposite each other and "read" each other's faces with your hands.'

Dylan walked his hand down an imaginary face.

'I put my hand lower and she didn't say anything. I travelled under her top, over her bra. Her breast felt like an ice-pack – that kind of consistency – only it wasn't cold, it was warm. And her nipple – '

'Stop!'

'What? We're just talking.'

'Oh – as long as we're just *talking*.' I grinned. 'Have you touched any other *breasts* . . . since Fleur?' I liked the way he called them breasts. It seemed politer somehow.

Dylan shook his head.

'You could touch mine.' It was the strangest thing. To hear myself saying something I hadn't thought through. There was no laughing now. I was aware of our breathing, and how hot and clammy the room was. I moved towards Dylan and he moved back. He actually rolled backwards to get away from me. He said, 'Are you rampant – or what?'

Just as my heart was imploding, a noise exploded from the garage next door.

'What's that?' Dylan asked.

I couldn't look at him. 'Bird. I think.'

Healing Properties

The noise settled down and was now recognisable as a car engine.

Dylan frowned. 'Someone needs a muffler.'

I squeezed past him and ran outside, across the porch to the garage. The dune buggy looked shiny and tantalising. Bird was under the bonnet.

'Holy spark plugs!' I cried. 'You did it!'

Bird shuffled backwards and turned to smile at me, but his smile died as soon as he saw Dylan in the doorway. He did his fitty thing, brushing his chin into his neck, looking up at me. Dylan wheeled in. He was doing his flash push where he just jammed his hands down once and let the momentum carry him forward. I guess it was the equivalent of strutting.

'What's he doing here?' Bird's voice was brittle. He was holding a wrench – it would have been menacing if it had been anyone other than Bird.

'Neville's making us clean up the house.'

'What's he doing with that?' Bird nodded to Fraser's notebook. He came forward and snatched it from Dylan's lap. Dylan held his hands up and murmured, 'Whoa! White flag.' In that second he sounded like Craig.

Bird climbed into the dune buggy and sat in the driver's seat. He rested Fraser's notebook on the wheel and started flipping through the pages, occasionally glancing up to shoot Dylan a look that was half contempt and half fear and wholly intriguing.

I nudged Dylan. 'Context please.' He didn't answer. He just rocked a little. I couldn't read his face. All I knew was that it was getting darker.

Bird kept his head down. He had a protective hand across his binoculars. I flashed on Olive saying – 'they trashed his binoculars' – and instinctively knew who 'they' were – not 'Janey and that', but Dylan and Craig, the comedy duo.

'You like seeing me in this, don't you?' Dylan drummed his hands on his chair arms. He was staring at Bird, and his chin was wobbling.

I touched his arm, 'Dylan – '

He shook me off. 'No – I saw his face at Orientation. He was smiling.'

Bird flipped the pages of the notebook harder and faster. And a smile started to grow on his face. Dylan reached for his crutches.

'Oh shit,' I whispered.

Dylan raised the crutch. Bird and I flinched. But then Dylan brought his crutch down limply to the floor and hung his head. He was silent for a moment and then he started head-banging, slowly. I crouched down to retrieve his crutch and put it back with its mate. Dylan looked up and his eyes were wet. He sighed audibly, and spoke in a heavy voice. 'Whatever, whatever. It's fair enough. I was a shit to him. I was a shit to him camp after camp. I was a shit to the lot of them. Fuck it.' He looked past my shoulder to his old victim. 'Just don't feel like you have to hide it, Bird. You know?'

Then he wheeled around and out. I opened the car door and got in next to Bird.

'He's not a bad guy,' I said, mostly to myself. 'He's just upset.'

Bird gripped the wheel. I closed my eyes and put my head on his shoulder and imagined us driving out of the garage and into the dunes. I saw it like it was the trailer to an action film. But in the final image it wasn't Bird sitting next to me; it was Dylan.

Bird passed me Fraser's notebook. 'Give him this.'

I held the notebook loosely.

'It shows where the salt lake is,' Bird nodded meaningfully. 'The salt lake that has healing properties.'

'I thought Trevor said Fraser was loopy-loo?'

'Fraser was a visionary,' Bird said firmly.

He got out and resumed fiddling under the bonnet.

I studied Fraser's map.

Bird's head popped to the side. 'Riley?'

'Yeah?'

'Can you keep the rest of Fraser's books for me? Hide them in here somewhere?'

'Sure . . . You don't really think – ' But the roar of the engine saved me from finishing. Bird closed the bonnet and beamed at me. Life was not complicated for Bird. Things were either good or bad. Roslyn said that to be a good person you had to believe in God, and to believe in God you had to be open as a child. You had to be open to believe in anything. I wasn't open. I was tight as a trap. I smoothed my hand over the notebook's dusty cover. Five minutes ago *Healing* was just a word in Norma's New Age lexicon. Now it seemed like a good prospect.

YESTERDAY'S GIRL

Sarita accosted me at lunchtime. 'Riley, you must tell me what you are going to do for the talent show.'

'Are you out of your curry-munching mind?'

Her face fell. 'I was hoping you would help me . . . come into the light.'

'What do you mean?'

'I mean I no longer wish to be "in the wings". I wish to be in the light.' She gripped her plaits. 'I thought you were going to help me metamorphose. You said so in your memory cross.'

'Oh God, I did, didn't I?' Suddenly I remembered the Hella Hot Oil. I seized Sarita by her shoulders and herded her back to the cabin; the whole time prating like a has-been on an infomercial. '*Are you tired of looking like yesterday's girl? Got fifteen minutes to radically change your appearance?*' Sarita trundled in front of me, delighted and excited.

I stopped at the kitchen for a cup of oats, one egg, a lemon, and two buckets of warm water, all courtesy of Olive. Back in the cabin I fixed my sarong around Sarita's neck and swivelled her chair away from the mirror. I mixed the ingredients up in Fleur's thermos and applied it to Sarita's face with a plastic spoon.

Sarita screwed up her nose. 'What is that?'

'It's organic,' I told her. 'Don't speak – it'll crack.'

I rubbed Vaseline into her eyebrows and began tweezing. Sarita squeaked at first but by the time I was onto her middle brow she had become beauty's bitch. She remained stoic throughout the haircut, despite what must have looked like random hacking. Her eyes widened at the growing pile of hair on the floor but she didn't speak. When my fingers accidentally lighted on her throat I could feel her pulse going like the clappers.

Haircutting is a meditative act. As I worked away I thought about Dylan's accident, and what Bird had said about the salt lake.

'Sarita,' I started. 'Do you remember when Trevor was talking about the salt lake?'

She nodded.

'Do you think that it's true that it has healing properties?'

Sarita considered this. She wobbled her head inconclusively.

'I wonder if Neville would let us go there? Say, as a special excursion?' I combed some stray hairs and snipped them diagonally. 'I bet if enough of us wanted to he'd let us go. What do you think? I think I'll ask him. It can't hurt to ask, right?'

Sarita said, 'Unnn hs isssian.' Her facemask cracked just a fraction.

'Wait.' I wiped the goo off with a flannel. 'What was that?'

'I said you could do a petition.'

Sarita had that worried look again. 'I feel different. I feel like something is missing.'

'Well, you look gorgeous,' I told her. 'Goodbye extra-curricular Asian nerd.' I swung her chair around. 'Hello Hindi Honey.'

'Oh, my,' Sarita breathed.

Her hair sat just below her chin. It framed her face and brought her fine features into light. Her hair was almost space-age in its shiny, solid perfection. But it was going to necessitate a whole new wardrobe. I trawled through her clothes, making reject-button sound effects the whole while.

'No, no, no,' I fretted. 'It's all so *Baptist.*'

'I don't understand,' said Sarita.

'You need a *trousseau*. That's French for fuck-clothes.'

'Riley. I said nothing earlier because I didn't want to alienate you with my intellect, but I *parlez-vous*,' Sarita said. 'The French do not have a word for . . .'

'Go on, say it!' I dared her.

Sarita zipped her lips.

'Every language has its limitations,' I said airily.

I looked at my clothes strewn all over the floor. 'It's a shame you're so tiny. Unless – ' I found my peasant blouse and tossed it to her. 'Put this on.'

Sarita obeyed. She looked like she'd stepped into a muu-muu.

'Wear it with the silver belt,' I suggested. I walked around her in a circle. 'Better. Now you just need some tights.'

I found my scissors again and cut the sleeves off my Goth Lolita dress. Sarita gasped. 'What are you doing?'

'Re-fashioning.' I passed the sleeves to her. 'Wear these like leggings.'

Sarita stepped into them. I walked around her again, nodding slowly. 'That's good,' I smiled. 'No shoes with this outfit – okay?' Sarita was staring in the mirror, swishing her skirt, beaming. I lay back on the bed. 'And now, my work is done.'

Fleur waltzed in with a volleyball under her arm. When she saw Sarita she dropped the ball. 'Wow.' She turned to me. 'Did you do that?'

I sat up, leaning on my elbows. 'Why – you want some work done?'

'No,' Fleur sputtered unconvincingly.

Sarita was experimenting with my eyeliner now, drawing artful curlicues on her temples. She turned to me. 'What do you think?'

I heard myself saying, 'My friend, my friend, I have taught you well.' A little bell went off somewhere in my head but I chose to ignore it.

PETITION

The afternoon was gorgeous, all golden and hazy with a blue still sky that looked like it had been freshly painted. I sat on the smokers' bench with Fraser's notebook and watched the Bronzewings' volleyball match. It almost looked like fun. *They* were laughing anyhow. Fleur was in the umpire's chair, her hand never far from the whistle. A couple of times I saw her look my way with a half-smile on her face. It crossed my mind that she might be trying to befriend me. The idea wasn't as repellent as it once had been. Maybe I *had* been infected. My hand marked the page with the map to the salt lake. The symbol for the lake was small and red, and shaped like a kidney bean. I touched the spot and felt its pull. I put Fraser's notebook to one side and took out my own bamboo-covered one. I wrote: *'Petition. In the interests of salvation and personal healing, we, the undersigned Honeyeaters, request permission to visit the salt lake. If not tomorrow then the day after.'*

Sarita and Bird were on my side; the twins were malleable, but Fleur, Richard and Ethan would require craftiness. I tackled Fleur first. She looked from the page to me and frowned.

'What's this?'

'A petition.'

She read and then pushed the page aside with the back of her hand. 'I don't want to go into the desert. It's too hot. It makes my hair frizzy.'

'If you sign, I'll cut your hair and frizz will be your friend.'

Fleur squinted around as if we were being watched. She hesitated, then picked up the pen and signed with a flourish.

Ethan and Richard were playing chess on one of the picnic tables. I approached with my happy-camper face on high. 'Have you heard?' I bubbled. 'Sarita's getting *Live Fresh* to film the talent show.'

'What?' Richard and Ethan looked up from their game.

'Yeah – she's contacted the host and everything. The only thing is – ' I leaned in with the petition. 'She has to get everyone's permission.'

Ethan rocked excitedly. 'Way cool! I love that show. You know that Candid Christians segment? It's so funny.'

Richard brought his queen home. 'Checkmate. Where do we sign?'

I saved Craig until last. I hadn't spoken to him since the roundabout. All my pointed looks seemed to bounce right off him. He was impervious. He galumphed around camp with his big, sexy legs and his killer smile, breaking hearts like old people break wind, that is to say, *a lot*. Every night his voice rose up above the campfire, rich and tremulous, and stirring. It was hard to hate him when he sang. He still tried with Dylan too – every activity, no matter how physical, he would come up to Dylan and encourage him to take part. I was getting sucked in. Floundering in the face of his . . . well, his face. I almost wondered if his shoving Bird was an aberration. But then I'd hear him speak and know that yes, everything came easily to him, everything except humility.

I cornered him outside the counsellors' annexe.

'Hey,' I said.

'Hey.'

Concentrate, I told myself. I too would be impervious.

'Would you sign this petition for me?'

He read it, then looked up at me. 'Why?'

'I just thought it would be fun.'

'They won't be able to swing it. Off-site activities are set months before we even get here.' Craig shrugged and you could tell he thought he was making a grand gesture. 'Sure, I'll sign it if you want, Riley. Whatevs.'

He signed, but when I tried to get the pen back, he kept hold of it. Tugging ensued. I gave up. 'This is corny,' I said. Craig stared at me, his eyes dark and sly.

'What?' I snapped.

He trailed a finger down my arm. 'I was wondering if you wanted to – '

I shook him off. 'Been there, done that, according to the rumours.'

'Hey – I didn't say that. It was Fleur.' He smiled stupidly and did a quick crotch-adjustment (re-crotching, Chloe calls it).

I stared at him, unimpressed. 'Itchy?'

He laughed again but something in his eyes had changed and suddenly he didn't look so alpha dog. He moved his mouth around and tugged on his shorts.

I arched an eyebrow, looked from his crotch to his face. 'If it's crabs, you'll have to shave your pubes off. Maybe Fleur will help you.' I waved the petition at him and started walking backwards. 'Thanks for signing. *Laters.*'

A Little Salvation

The Bronzewings moved off the court and the twins started mucking around with the volleyball. Sarita joined them. Her hair hardly moved as she bounced around. I don't know what my face was saying to them but one minute I was on the sidelines and the next minute I felt the ball in my stomach. 'Oof!' I doubled over, trapping it in my arms.

'Chuck it back!' Lisa yelled.

'Come on, Riley!' Sarita was grinning and waving her arms.

A voice came from the other side, 'Chuck it to me!' That was Richard. What an invitation! I threw the ball at him as hard as I could. He threw it back just as hard, and then, somehow, I was playing volleyball with the twins and Richard and Ethan and Sarita. And the weird thing was – it *was* fun. I didn't mind that my soft hands were getting all banged up because it felt *good* to thump the ball like that. It felt *good* to leap and dive. And when I aced a shot it felt . . . *great*. After twenty minutes of urgent spiking we had drawn a crowd. I played up to them. I was theatrical –

weeping when I missed a shot, spinning when I made one. I danced on my toes and embraced the cheers. Neville was my number one fan. He was beaming, rolling his fist and chanting, 'Go Ri-ley, Go Ri-ley!'

After a killer finish the good counsellor trotted up with cold water and compliments. 'Nice game.' He clapped his hand on my aching shoulder. 'It's great to see you participating, Riley.'

I felt momentarily shocked – was *that* what I'd been doing? Then I saw how I could work my perceived cooperation to my advantage. I bought up the petition. Neville looked at me like I was crazy. 'Absolutely not! The salt lake isn't even accessible.'

'It is! There's a fire road. I've got . . . I've seen the map.'

'Riley. Let me tell you something about structure. Have you heard of structure? Well, structure is important. Do you want to know why it's important? Because, Riley, without structure, everything falls apart. Do you understand what I'm saying?'

'Not really.'

'Even if I thought it was a good idea for you to go to the salt lake – which I don't – we already have your off-site activity planned for tomorrow. We're going white-water rafting at the falls.'

'But what about after that?'

'No. I can't even entertain the thought.'

'Trevor said it was a healing lake,' I put in.

Neville smiled at Trevor's name. 'Never mind what Trevor said.' He looked at me, almost fondly. For a minute I thought

190

he might ruffle my hair. 'Riley, am I right in thinking that you want to take Dylan to the salt lake so that he can be "cured"?'

'No.' I ducked and shrugged. It sounded stupid out loud.

'Come on.' Neville closed the subject with a sanctimonious smile. 'How are you going with the house?'

'We still have to do the second room.'

'You can finish up in the morning before the falls excursion. Unless you mind missing The Word.'

'I don't mind.'

'No – ' Neville looked at me sideways. 'I didn't think you would.'

Dylan wheeled out of his room, plugged in and staring across the plain to the latest round of jumping, sweating, shrieking, high-fiving, fully active campers. Suddenly I felt a burning injustice on his behalf. Fuck structure! It was okay for Neville, flouncing around in his high pants. And Roslyn, doing her mad rockin' pelvis dance. And Anton, leading yet another troop of Mallees into the scrub. It was okay for *them*. But all Dylan could do was watch and pretend he didn't want any part of it. I knew that was what he was doing because that was what I had always done. We were the Mutards – and after all we had been through, well, what was so wrong with a little Salvation?

I tried to give Neville the petition but he wouldn't take it.

'Please,' I beseeched him. 'It's important.'

'It's not going to happen. We'd need permission, there's no vehicle – '

'Maybe Trevor could take us?'

'Sorry.' Neville started to walk away.

I had one card left – blackmail. I blurted, 'I'll tell everyone about you two . . . you and Trevor . . .'

Neville paused. He took a sharp breath in and frowned at the sky. Then he gave me a funny, stilted smile. 'I have nothing to hide from God,' he said. He reached over and put his hand on my shoulder. 'Okay?'

'Okay,' I muttered, stirring the dirt with my shoe. 'Sorry.'

He started to walk away and I thought of something else. 'Can I make a phone call?' I asked him.

'Riley . . .' Neville sighed. 'Okay – just this once.'

In his office Neville passed me the phone and then he just stood there. I gave him a look. He gave me a look back and kind of rolled his shoulders and took himself out to the hall.

Chloe's phone went straight to voicemail.

'It's me,' I said. 'Are you screening? Pick up, pick up, pick up. Okay. Obviously I am still in Hell. I'm sorry you had to get up early all for nothing. And I'm *traumatised* about Ben's party . . .' I drawled. 'I'm puncturing my skin with a blunt compass as we speak.' I waited. She didn't pick up. 'Okay, Chlo, I've gotta go. I'll be back Sunday night for deprogramming. *Arghhh, help!*' I held the receiver out and shrieked twice before hanging up.

Neville's drawer was open a crack – I opened it all the way. There were hundreds of Jesus badges inside. Hundreds! I grabbed one and put it in my bag. Then I noticed a set of keys, labelled *Fraser*. I weighed them in my hand. My finger traced the VW insignia and I could have smacked myself.

Why was I trying so hard? I didn't need a petition. I didn't need *permission*. We did have a vehicle – the dune buggy! With no lesson in hot-wiring necessary thank you very much. I spun myself around and around and around in the chair until I felt too sick to be excited.

Aces

The prospect of the salt lake expedition enhanced my otherness. I was not like them – the other campers, the coloured balls. I was strong. I had purpose. I could make things happen. At dinner I shuffled down the table until I was next to Dylan.

'I have something cool to tell you.'

He held his hand up to calm me down. 'Fleur already told me about the petition.'

'You talked to Fleur? When?'

Dylan smiled. 'When you were playing volleyball.'

I winced. 'You saw that?'

The knowledge that Dylan had seen me being 'physically active' sent me into High Cringe. That meant he'd seen all my flesh sliding around and my face going blueberry. He might have even seen me laughing with the twins – over a ball!

'You were getting into it.' Dylan smiled again, but it wasn't a sly smile. 'It was nice to see you having fun. Different.'

'Shaddup.' I waved him away. 'I was playing along. I was trying to infiltrate so that I could get – ' I uncurled my hand and showed him the key to the dune buggy. 'This.'

Dylan looked confused for a moment, then the wrinkles on his brow straightened out. 'Does that thing really work?' He asked idly, as if he didn't care about the answer.

I nodded. 'So – tomorrow we're going to the salt lake.'

Dylan said nothing. He poked at his dinner. He dragged his fork through the gravy, making little swirling patterns.

'The salt lake,' I reminded him. 'In the desert, the one with the *healing powers*.'

Dylan put his fork down. 'I might have a conflict of interest.'

'What do you mean?'

'I don't think I can believe in the salt lake and still believe in God.'

'Fuck off,' I said. 'If you can suspend your disbelief for arks, or people getting turned into pillars of salt, or bloody great kippers falling from the sky, then I don't see why you can't do it for me.'

'Oh, I'm doing it for you now, am I?' Dylan smiled. He drummed his fists on his thighs. I put my hands over his and drummed with him, but I was too excited. I really thumped him.

'Shit,' I said. 'Can you feel that?'

He laughed. 'No.'

I kept drumming a complicated beat.

That night's movie was a Good Word documentary about cults. Three hours of Orange People, Waco and Reverend Jim

Jones. Dylan and I started laughing during the segment on the Manson Family. He was so psycho – *'My eyes light fires in your homes!'* – and his girls looked so skanky – with their lank hair and acne, their miniskirts, lovebeads and swastikas. They kept showing the same still of the Spahn Ranch where the Manson Family had lived. It was dusty and spooky-familiar. Every time the voiceover said the word 'Spahn' Dylan would counter with 'Spirit'. In the re-enactments showing the Family's chill-time – ie, singing around a camp-fire – Charles Manson had a guitar, and whenever they showed a close-up of him, Dylan would whisper, 'Craig'. We chuckled into our sleeves and suffered terse looks from Anton. The video ended with a big plea for God-ness and that old chestnut about not worshiping false idols – oh, irony! But I was in too good a mood to dispute it.

That night I lay awake in bed listening to the Boobook owl. I was thinking about the salt lake. I had no idea what it looked like. What I imagined was not unlike the illustrations in *Utopia*. I pictured a mirage: after miles of sand an oasis would spring up, complete with palm trees and parrots and big personality flowers. The salt lake would be pale green – opalescent – and the salt crystals would sparkle in the sunlight. The water would feel cool, maybe even carbonated. Once Dylan and I were immersed we wouldn't be able to feel our bodies. We'd surrender to the lake's drift, its pulsing currents and tingle-essence. Dylan's crutches would float away like driftwood. And we'd laugh. We'd sink our heads under the water and hold our breath till one hundred.

And when we came back out we'd be different. Dylan would be able to walk and I'd be able to cry.

When I finally fell asleep I had weird, foggy, fumbling dreams. In one Counsellor Neville had wet his pants. He kept saying, 'It's okay, everybody, it's just water,' and smiling like a child. In another Dylan was dancing and he moved like a . . . well, like a dream.

ON THE FIFTH DAY

WONDERFULLY MADE

On the morning of Day Five cabin three awoke to heavy banging on the door. Fleur slipped out of bed to open it and there stood Roslyn in a pair of spectacularly bedazzled bib overalls. 'I'm bringing the breakfast bugle to each of you . . . personally!' She drew the bugle to her lips and smiled around the mouthpiece. I braced for the squall. Fleur gawped at me. I shook my head. Sarita huddled up against the wall with her hands over her ears. Roslyn blew and blew. Finally, she lowered the bugle and smiled like an axe-murderer. 'The thought for the morning is: *I am fearfully and wonderfully made!*' Roslyn took a bow. On her way back up she noticed the lipstick-y shroud tacked to the mirror. She reached for it, and rasped, 'Which one of you found this?'

Sarita was shaking her head and mouthing '*don't*' but I wanted to see what would happen. I put my hand up. 'I did.'

'And you didn't think to hand it in?' Roslyn's voice climbed the walls. 'You thought instead that it would be fun to soil it with your . . . ' Her mouth was pursed in disgust as she searched for the right word. '*Whore-paint!*'

'Ew!' Fleur reeled back.

'I only kissed it,' I said innocently. 'I love Jesus.'

Roslyn scrunched the shroud in her fist and stormed out. After the door had stopped quaking, Fleur smiled. 'She *hates* you.' Then: 'When are you going to do my hair?'

I could feel Roslyn eyeballing me all through breakfast. I told Dylan about her visit. 'Did she bugle at *Casa Mutard*?' I asked.

He nodded. 'She told me she was fearfully and wonderfully made.'

'We all are,' I drawled.

'Oh *sure*.' Dylan looked down at his legs and then up at me. 'You shouldn't have taken her shroud. People have to have things to believe in.'

'It was just lipstick.' Dylan looked at me and I felt ashamed. It was a shitty thing to do. Unfeeling. It was like turning someone's lucky horseshoe upside down, or ripping the last page out of a library book. 'All right,' I said. ' I'll go and apologise.'

Roslyn didn't make it easy for me. She was so wounded. Her brow was rippled like sand at low tide. Call me the wrinkle-bringer. I knew that expression too well. She could have been Norma, the time she figured out that I'd nicked her credit card. Or Dad, the time he'd found me puking in Mr Ping's poinsettias. Or – and I didn't like remembering this because it wasn't a Good Memory – she could have been Mum.

I was eight and Freya, Queen of Grade Three, was coming

over to play. I was supposed to tidy my room but I elected
to trash it instead. I had a frenzied half hour of pulling things
from drawers, imagining Freya's look of awe as she stepped
over Power Rangers and Dr Seuss. My Grade Three logic said
that this would make me memorable. Mum was so angry she
almost hit me. She brought her fist to my face and then
opened it at the last minute. Pouf! It was scary, knowing
I could make her that mad. Later, Mum told me it takes
forty-three muscles to frown. She jabbed a finger at a deep
line in the middle of her forehead – 'You see that?' she said.
'That one's got your name on it.' Dad never got angry
like Mum did. Norma says Dad has a blue aura. Mine is red.
Mum's would have been red too.

'I'm sorry I ruined your shroud,' I told Roslyn. 'If there's
anything I can do to make it up to you . . .' It was just a line
but Roslyn caught it and hung on.

'As a matter of fact, there is. I want you to think really
hard, Riley. Think about what you believe in. Think about
what God means to you. And then, I want you to express
the results of your ruminations at the talent show. It can be
in song form, or a dance, or a dramatic oration.'

I gave her a scarecrow's smile. I heard myself say, 'Sure,
that sounds neat.' *Sure? Neat?* I staggered back to the
Honeyeaters' table, reached for Dylan's toast and decimated
it. He was smiling. 'That bad?'

All I could do was shake my head. 'Jay-sus. You *so* owe me.'

PAST LIFE

Nothing could get to me that morning. Not Roslyn's miffedness, not Richard and Ethan's creation theory breakdown, not Fleur alternating between nagging me about her hair and bitching at me for taking the last muffin. Even Anton's order that I help out in the kitchen didn't faze me. I rolled up my sleeves and stood next to Olive at the sink. She washed and I dried. I must have been radiating happiness because now and then she'd steal a look and then it was as if my happiness was contagious because Olive would seem to rise inside her apron and a second later she'd burst out with some nutty insight.

'I saw a comet last night. I counted over twenty deep sky objects. A nebulae, a star cluster, a quasar – '

I studied her but I wasn't really listening. 'Olive, how did you and Bird get to be . . . you and Bird?' I asked her.

'Mum used to design satellites and Dad teaches theology.' Olive brought a plate up for closer inspection. 'Bird says it's the best of both worlds. Lots of hypotheticals in our house.'

I wanted Bird and Olive on my team. Absolutely.

'This is confidential,' I whispered. 'Dylan and I are going into the desert today. We're going to try to find Fraser's salt lake.'

Olive clapped a rubber-gloved hand over her mouth. She squeaked through her fingers. 'That is so exciting.'

'It's all thanks to Bird. We're taking the dune buggy.'

Olive took her hand away, and spat out suds. She looked around and lowered her voice. 'You'll need supplies. Food and water.'

'Can you sort something out?'

'It would be an honour.'

'Tell Bird to meet us at the garage in an hour – I don't want to raise suspicion among the Honeyeaters.'

'Don't tell them – or they'll all want to go.'

Olive seemed much wiser than her years. Norma would have called her an 'old soul'. She who once told me that in a past life I was the town prostitute – they put me in stocks and pelted me with old fruit. Ah, Norma!

Cultural Anthropology

Neville came with us to open up Fraser's house. I watched the bunch of keys crash against his hip and smiled. I knew why their clank and jangle sounded different. I kept my hand in my pocket on the key to the dune buggy and wondered what kind of music it would make on its own.

Someone had collected the op-shop boxes in the night but Fraser's journals were safe in the garage for Bird. The mysterious cleaner-upper had also opened the curtains and swept the porch and now Fraser's house had all the hallmarks of a 'cottage charmer'. The second room, his bedroom, was *almost* presentable. It was dusty and there were still book colonies all over the floor but it lacked the 'local tip' décor of the first room.

'Shouldn't take you long,' Neville said. He passed me his watch. 'Get back by noon so you've got enough time to clean up before the falls.'

Dylan spoke up. 'I don't want to go to the falls. There's no point. I'll just be sitting there.'

I jumped in. 'I don't want to go either. I practically drowned when we did the canoeing.'

'What are you proposing?' Neville asked.

My mind raced. I needed a plausible, admirable lie so that Neville could let us off and still feel like he was doing his job.

'We could spend the time reflecting,' I offered. 'We could work on something for the talent show. I know I said it as a joke but now I've made this promise to Roslyn . . .'

Neville looked bemused. He didn't *quite* believe me. But he wanted to. Need is not quite belief, but sometimes it'll do.

'I guess there's no reason why you can't stay back,' Neville said. 'It is beautiful country though.'

'I'm not that into nature,' I said, smiling slyly at Dylan. 'I'm a city girl.'

'Gotcha.' Neville kicked a leg towards the door. I got the feeling that he was lingering, almost as if he wanted to dispatch his counsellor duties and hang with the bad kids. He was okay, Neville, for a glass-eyed, super-gay, good-intentioned God-botherer. He slapped the door frame. 'Have *fu*-un . . .' and his final advice swept the floor like a lyrebird's tail, '. . . safe fun.'

Dylan and I locked eyes and sing-songed back. '*We will.*'

We worked fast, emptying drawers and filling rubbish bags. I no longer felt weird about poking around Fraser's personal stuff. We weren't campers doing shit-work. We were cultural anthropologists searching for artefacts.

On the bedside table I found an old photograph. *Nicholas and Rose Fraser, Wedding Day, 1964.* They were standing in front of the house, unsmiling. Fraser looked wiry. He was a young-old man in his suit and hat and bow-tie. His wife wore a white dress and carried a sheaf of long grass and peacock feathers. I stared at the photo for a while. Rose Fraser. She had my name, and she was fat like me. Plump. Comfy. Big-boned.

'When did Fraser die?' I asked.

Dylan didn't answer. He was fiddling with an old cassette player. Suddenly the room was full of horns. The singer had a mighty timbre. Dylan pulled a swift three-sixty. He was singing along, using everything – his voice, his face, his hands.

'What is this old people's music?' I shouted above the din.

Dylan managed to shout back, 'Neville Special,' without missing a beat. 'It's Tom Jones – "Delilah".'

Tom Jones wailed and Dylan wailed with him. Then there was a hiss and a pop. Some smoke rose up. The amplifier had died but Dylan kept singing. Later, at the naming of the dune buggy, Dylan would start singing again. We needed a name to suit the mission, something sexy . . . and dangerous. Why, why, why *not* Delilah? The name suited her so much it was perfect.

CONVERSATION WITHOUT WORDS

All morning Dylan and I talked like we were in contest. We talked like a tug-of-war. We talked like a toboggan. I told him about Chloe, the bunker book and the bus ticket. He told me about how he ended up in Trevor's ute.

'Fleur wanted a blue rose. I know she wrote it as a joke – a blue rose is like a black orchid – but I got it in my head that if I could get her one . . .' He stopped and smiled ruefully. 'She'd chuck Craig and come sit on my lap. There's no florist in Nhill, but there was a newsagents. I bought that notebook. Your notebook. And well . . . you saw the pictures. I tried to draw a blue rose. Then I realised the whole thing was stupid. I had some money left over so I bought a bottle of brandy and holed up in an empty shop and the rest is history.'

'Fleur's not as bad as I thought she was.'

'She's okay,' Dylan said. 'But she's not worthy of a blue rose.'

'Well, it's mine now.'

Dylan went on. 'I was shitty about Craig too. After February 2 he was the only one who didn't come on with the bright fake bullshit. He visited me in rehab, we played cards. I thought we'd be okay. But it's context, isn't it? I look at him here and all I see is triumph. It's Fleur. And it's his fucking legs.' Dylan ran his hands up and down his jeans, fast, and I imagined them sparking. 'Drugs,' he deadpanned. 'Sometimes I invent things. Craig's a good guy, the best. But that doesn't mean he can't be a prick as well.'

'I've seen a few pricks in my time,' I joked.

Dylan didn't laugh. I was sitting in Fraser's old rocking chair. I rocked back and forth. 'Um. That was one of Chloe's.'

'That's not you.'

I really, really wanted to believe him but the graffiti was on the wall. Not only *Fatgirlsaregrateful* but also *Are you rampant*? As if he'd read my mind, Dylan said, 'Sorry I called you rampant. I was confused about the Craig thing.'

'There's no Craig thing.' I took a breath. Dylan was saying he didn't want to go there – and that made sense. Take a fat girl like me and a broken boy like him – how could we be anything *but* friends? And now because he'd shared something, I wanted to share something back.

'I have Mum's memory trunk at home. I used to look at it all the time, but I haven't looked at it for ages. Not since we moved. It's like if I open it I'll just want to climb in and close the lid and breathe her air, until I'm full of her. But I can never be full of her – you know what I mean?'

'It's like every scrap of information I get is just a tease about all the stuff I'll never know.' I stopped. My throat was dry. I wanted a cigarette, not to smoke, just to hold.

'Oh no,' Dylan warded me off with his hands. 'Don't cry.'

'I won't,' I assured him. 'I don't. In the trunk there was this program for Mum's high school musical. She wasn't starring or anything – she was just in the chorus. I can see her up the back, singing, mucking around. Anyway, there were messages all through the program. From guys, and they were all, like, filthy.'

'Conclusion,' I sat forward. 'I think *she* might have been rampant. But I don't know what I am.'

I wasn't expecting it when Dylan leaned in and kissed me. We kissed for ages. It felt like we were continuing our conversation only without words. We kept our hands half-out like toddlers when they run, because the laying of hands on body parts would bring about a reality that I don't think either of us was ready for yet.

DRESSED!

Right on cue, Bird stuck his head in. He had a jerry can with him, full of petrol siphoned from Anton's car.

'You're a legend,' I gushed.

'I wish I could come on her maiden voyage,' Bird said. 'There's treasure out there. You might see a Crimson Chat. I'd give my eyes to see a Crimson Chat.' He passed me a paper bag. 'From Olive.' I passed the bag to Dylan and he held up items and mimicked Neville:

'Bottled water. One packet of Monte Carlos. Two Fuji apples. Toilet paper. One packet of Band-Aids. Matches. Candle. One bottle of champagne.'

'What?' I squeaked.

'True.' Dylan sctutinised the label. 'Two thousand and seven. A very good year.'

'Olive is a legend too,' I told Bird. He looked proud.

'What do you think of Delilah for a name?' Dylan asked him. It was the first time he'd spoken directly to Bird since their face-off in the garage. I wondered how Bird would take it. He took it straight. He meditated on the name, and mouthed it a couple of times, testing it out. Finally he nodded. 'Okay.' Then he said something strange. 'In a way, I don't mind if she doesn't come back.'

'What do you mean?' I asked him.

'Well, Fraser went into the desert to die, so in a way it would be good if Delilah died there too.'

I patted his arm. 'No one's going to die, Bird. She'll be fine.'

'Changes occur in the desert,' Bird said vaguely. He took a step backwards, gave us a funny little kung-fu bow and left the building.

Dylan was silent for a long time. I wondered if he was thinking about Bird, and the past, and how when one thing shifts, everything else shifts with it. I was thinking about Fraser's notebooks, the sum of his life, and how good it was they had somewhere to go. After Mum died, Dad said I should take what I wanted; the rest was going to go. I never asked where, and he never said. I didn't know what to take. Nothing could replace her. In the end I took some of her jewellery, and books, and her most fabulous caftan and put them in her memory trunk.

I opened Fraser's closet door and touched the clothes.

'I wonder when his wife died.'

'Maybe she didn't. Maybe she left him.'

'She wouldn't have left him,' I said softly.

Dylan gave me a look.

'Mothballs always make me sentimental,' I joked.

At the back of the closet something made my eyes pop.

'Oh. Wow,' I breathed.

'Skeleton?'

'Sort of.' I reached in. Wrapped in plastic, looking almost like a museum exhibit, were Fraser and Rose's wedding clothes. I took the dress out of its sheath and I posed in front of the mirror, holding it out in front of me.

'This might even fit.'

'Should we be going soon?' Dylan's voice was edgy. 'If we're going to go we should go.'

'Just wait a sec.' I wriggled out of my blouse and kicked my jeans off. I didn't even think about the fact that Dylan was going to see me in my boulder bra and Wonderpants.

'Hey Riley?'

'Wait.' I put the ancient dress on over my head. It was silk-lined and it floated over my skin. I stood in front of the mirror. 'This is so cool.' I showed Dylan my back. 'Can you zip me up?'

'Come closer.'

The zip wouldn't go past my waist. No corset.

'Backless,' I affirmed. 'How do I look?'

Dylan looked from the photograph to me. 'Stop smiling,' he said. But I couldn't and he couldn't and then he was tearing the plastic off Fraser's suit and it took a bit longer for him, because he had to wobble around on his crutches, plus we were laughing so that got in the way and I couldn't help noticing that his legs were white as white could be with hardly any hair, and he had lots of old scars from cigarettes, from pens, from compasses but it didn't matter because Dylan and I were going to the salt lake and we were totally dressed for the occasion.

ACCIDENTS 1 & 2

All cars have their quirks and Delilah was no exception. Bird had called her 'temperamental'. He said she'd only start in second gear, and might need external assistance. We determined that Dylan would take the wheel and use his crutch to keep the accelerator down. I'd push until Delilah was outside where we could – to use the parlance of revheads – 'really open her up'.

Dylan fixed himself behind the driver's seat. He turned the key and pumped the accelerator, but he couldn't seem to bring his hands down on the wheel. I looked up. The back of his neck had gone red. I called out to him. 'Everything okay?'

'Sorry. It's the first time I've been behind the wheel since . . . ' Dylan raked his hand through his hair. 'Give me a minute.'

The first accident happened at – or rather to – the camp boundary. Fraser's map hadn't said anything about a wire fence, but there it was. And I had pedal dyslexia.

'Slow down,' Dylan yelled.

'I'm trying to!' I yelled back.

'Fuuuucccck!' We ploughed through the fence.

Now we were on the Nhill road. We thundered on. Dylan was staring straight ahead and fondling his silver cross. I thought I heard him say, 'We are going to die.' But there was the wind and the engine sounded like Armageddon. On top of that I was laughing. Too much oxygen. Too much freedom. We were a devastation on four fat sand tyres. We almost missed the desert turnoff. Now the road went feral, the edges were soft and dangerous, but that only made me want to drive faster. We tore off down the fire road, grazing flora, scaring fauna, laughing like terrible hoons.

The second accident was a lot more serious.

Parallel Lines

When I opened my eyes all I could see was sky. For a while I only knew two words – blue sky – sky blue. Then the more pretentious adjectives came: surreal blue, Klee blue, Mum would have said Paul Newman blue. How long had I been out for? Where was I again? The sun seemed close, like I could reach up and volley it over the net of wispy clouds. I looked down and around to an army of trees. And rosellas! A flock burst from the branches like a paintball explosion and stunned me back to the situation at hand.

We were in the Little Desert. I'd been driving – too fast down the fire road. I'd spaced for a second, hit a pothole and Delilah had lost a wheel. Then we'd hit the tree. The red mallee bastard had a trunk as wide as a mini-van. I nearly hurled when I saw the dent in Delilah's bonnet. The wheel was back several metres in the sand, but everything else was in its place. Everything except Dylan and his wheelchair. Panic hit me like a bag of oranges – all over and everywhere at once. I had a moment of blindness, of tilt and trauma. I grabbed my bag, gathered the skirt of Rose's wedding dress and climbed out. On *terra firma* I rotated my arm like it was a compass that would point me in the right direction. Then I saw the tracks, parallel lines cut straight in the sand, going up and over a small hill. I walked between them, heart pounding.

Over the crest the land became crowded. Trevor said that the term 'desert' confused people, made them think there was nothing, when there was actually a whole world at work. Here, scrub rough as steel wool mixed with the most delicate flowers. Here, I took a step and a lizard as big as my foot shot under a piece of bark. There were grass trees – stunted, burned-black with hair worse than Roslyn's – and there were ghost trees, tall and twisted and haphazard. They reminded me of old people. Some of them even looked like old people with deep pockets in their skin, wise airs, and flakage.

The sun dipped. The sky became the near-night blue of shadows and stolen moments. Now the ground was firmer. The land had flattened out and Dylan's tracks were no longer visible. Here and there, I found little reflecting pools, and then at last I saw one great big one. The lake was a giant mirror reflecting a crazy-paving of tree and sky. Up ahead I saw a monster gum tree with wandering roots that looked like they'd waded right into the water and thought, *fuck it, let's stop here*. Dylan must have thought the same thing. He was in his chair, facing the water, a little way back from the edge.

WANTING

I tapped him on the shoulder. 'Hey Mutard.'

He turned and then wheeled all the way around. I saw a dozen looks cross his face, but the one that stayed was relief. 'Thank God, you're all right!' He was rubbing the heels of his hands on his wheels. His voice sounded raw. 'I tried to get help. I started off going back the way we came, but it was too sandy, so I thought I'd try another way. And then I just went whichever way I could. And ended up here.' He saw me smiling past his head. 'What?'

'Nice aspect.' I pointed to the lake. The sky had gone orangey-pink and the lake reflected the colours.

'There's something else,' Dylan said quickly. 'The lake. It's salty.'

'This must be it then.' I took Fraser's notebook out and tried to place the little red bean. It made sense – we were only a short way off the fire road and the little hill was marked. I squealed and kicked off my shoes and turned to Dylan. 'Let's do it.' I lifted my dress above my head and started in.

'Wow . . . It's *warm*.' The floor of the lake was silky-soft. I performed a slow twist, beckoning to him. 'Come on in, the water's fine!' The water *was* fine. It was better than fine. I took moon steps until it was up to my neck, and then I plunged. When I came back up, Dylan was still on the shore. I paddled towards him.

'What are you doing?'

'It's not going to work,' he said. But his voice was tentative. Hopeful.

'Come in anyway.' As soon as I said it, he knew – like I knew. Like I'd always known. There was no miracle. There was just wanting.

I floated on my back and closed my eyes. I let the water cover my ears so that all I could hear was hum. Then I opened my eyes to the huge gelato sky, swirling lemon and raspberry and pomegranate. I counted to ten then I looked back. Dylan was on his crutches coming towards me. He'd stripped off and was wearing only Fraser's bow-tie (slightly skewed), white boxers (rumpled) and a look of grim determination (cute). His face changed when he felt the water. He looked the same way he had in that photograph in Neville's office. And a thought rose up – *that* Dylan wouldn't have gone near me, but this one was waist-deep in a salt lake in the middle of the Little Desert. For me.

Repent Repent

This is what didn't happen:

1. Dylan didn't start spazzing out and speaking in tongues.
2. He didn't send his crutches like spears into the Never-Never.
3. He didn't float or sink or start to bawl.

He stayed in the shallows, watching the surface of the water while I did mermaid impressions, dolphin impressions; I gave good spray! Night fell quickly. I got out and put my dress back on over my wet skin, which was tingling just enough to make me feel like maybe, *maybe*, something crazy could happen.

Dylan scooched backwards until he was sitting next to me. He dried his legs carefully with the army blanket from Fraser's house, and he did his rearranging thing. Shifting his bum, lifting his legs up, letting them fall back down.

'Why do you do that?' I asked.

'Circulation.' He knocked on his thigh, clicking his

tongue. 'My pulled pins. It's like because I can't feel them, I have to take *more* care of them. They're like pets. Or those Tamagotchis. Or Sea Monkeys. You know – they're not really alive, but you have to treat them like they are.'

'When I was little I used to keep silkworms,' I told him. 'But we had a forty-degree day and I forgot to insulate their box, so they perished.'

'You are a cruel mistress.'

There were more stars in the Little Desert than I'd ever seen before and the more I looked the more I found. The sky was expanding. It made me feel loose, loquacious. With Dylan, my thoughts rolled out, easy as breathing.

'I used to think whenever someone died they became a star.'

'What do you think now?'

'Now I don't think.' I gnawed on a Monte Carlo. 'Now you can buy stars on the Internet.'

'I believe in Heaven,' Dylan said.

'I want to. I don't like to think of everything just stopping.' I scoffed another biscuit. And another one. I was working through the packet with all the grace of a wildebeest. 'But, I feel like if I go along with the idea of Heaven I have to go along with everything else.'

Dylan was quiet, so I went on.

'I used to see this homeless guy every day on the way to school. He'd camp out in the park near the train station. He had signs: *The End of the World is Nigh! Repent! Repent!* He had a tape recorder blasting out sermons – and he always wore earmuffs. We called him the Muffman – I know, very original. The story went that he used to be okay but then his wife and child died in a car accident. He was the one driving. So, he finds God, relinquishes his worldly goods, sleeps in a cardboard box under the Back Creek Bridge and tries to spread the Good Word. One morning he wasn't at the park. It turned out some kids had followed him and set his cardboard box on fire – while he was in it. You think this kind of thing doesn't happen but it does. I remember thinking the Muffman was *for* God, and God can see everything, so it was like God sanctioned it.'

'I don't think of it like that, like "sanctioning",' Dylan said, slow and serious. 'Your number's up when your number's up. I was under a tractor. I was that close to having my vitals crushed beyond repair. Makes you know what your vitals are, that's all.'

'When Mum – ' I stopped. I'd only just heard what he'd said. 'My mum was vital.'

I suddenly felt exhausted. I had so many questions. I could almost see them. They were sharp picks puncturing my brain.

We went quiet. We didn't have any answers.

Dylan found the champagne bottle, and sent the cork sky-high. He lifted it to his lips, took a great gulp.

'Do you think I'm fat?' I asked him.

He swallowed and wiped his mouth. 'I think you're beautiful.'

Trust Games

The candle was citronella. It smelled awful but it burned bright and kept the mosquitoes at bay. Dylan and I were sitting with the army blanket across our legs. Our hands were dancing under there. We were playing a new trust game. The rules were we had to be touching at all times. According to Neville's watch it was 10 pm and so far neither of us had mentioned where we were, or what we'd done, or why we'd done it. I felt like this was our place – and the world didn't really exist outside it.

Finally I broached the subject. 'What do you think they'll do to us?'

'I don't know,' Dylan said. 'Neville's not that big on confrontation . . . you may have noticed that he likes to keep things nice.'

'But . . . what about him and Trevor?'

Dylan grinned and shook his head. 'Ah, Nev-and-Trev.'

And there I was thinking I had some hot gossip. 'What, is it like some open secret?'

'Sort of. The older kids know, and some of the parents but this camp is like *relief* to them – a cheapo week without little Johnny and Mary, you know?'

'I thought you weren't allowed to have gay Christians.'

'These are modern times.'

I put on my professor voice. 'Or is it that we are living in a post-God society?'

'Do you really think these things, or do you just say them?'

'I don't know. The second one.' I smiled. 'I know what my mum would say. *Jay*-sus!'

Dylan was concentrating, pushing tulle around. 'They'll probably just tell us we can't come back. My mother will cry. She's good at that. She cried on and off the whole way up here. She won't look at my legs anymore. When Craig was showing us my cabin, Mum kept looking at his legs and going, "*When did you get so tall? Was he always this tall?*" And then when he left she cried again.'

I grimaced. 'I'm sure Dad and Norma just want to put me in a shipping container until I turn eighteen.'

'I'd rather that,' Dylan said. 'I get too much input. Special needs.' He sighed. 'Parents suck.'

'Arse and dick.' I said it like Chloe would: stoic, fateful.

Dylan was impressed. 'That's filthy.'

'How are your legs?'

'The same.' Dylan lit two cigarettes and passed me one. 'I don't mind. I didn't think it was going to work.'

'Me neither,' I lied. 'I was only hoping.' Hope is not belief either.

Dylan laughed shortly. 'Really. I mean, imagine if it *had* worked. It would have been a circus. I would have had to go on *Today Tonight* – I'd be the Salt Lake Miracle Boy. Still. It'd be cool not to have to hear about stem cell research and advanced physio.'

'Do you do much physio?'

Dylan didn't answer. I wondered if I was pushing it, pursuing a line that he didn't want brought into any kind of relief. But then he answered with a shrug. 'I used to. I used to be eager and positive and do all the exercises but nothing ever changed.'

'But isn't it supposed to take ages?'

'Yeah, but it makes me angry. I don't like getting angry. I like to keep in control. I like knowing what's around the corner.'

'We're the opposite. I like surprises and I have no control.'

Dylan looked at me.

I looked at him.

He moved into me and we kissed. I kept my eyes closed the whole time. After a while, Dylan drew his head back. 'Can you feel that?' he whispered.

I could feel lots of things, but one thing in particular.

'Do you mean what I think you mean?'

Dylan giggled.

I giggled.

'On my leg,' I whispered.

'No, no!' Dylan coughed. 'I was referring to the change in temperature.'

'You were not!'

He laughed and we went back under.

'It's still there,' I whispered again.

Dylan said, 'Mmm.'

'We can't leave it like that.' I wriggled out from under him. Then I started to act. I pouted and let my fingers flutter around my breasts – all those moves you see on *MTV*.

Dylan didn't respond. Eventually I sat up. 'I can't work under these conditions.'

'You don't have to do all that,' he said. 'We don't *have* to do *anything*.'

'Don't you want to?'

Dylan didn't answer. I checked under the blanket and came back pouting. 'It's gone.'

'See?' Dylan folded his arms under his head, looking proud. 'I can control *some* things. Not a lot of seventeen-year-old guys can say that.'

'I'm insulted,' I sniffed. 'Sex is supposed to be fun, you know.'

Dylan looked out to the lake. 'We had sex counselling at the hospital – complete with a video of a "normal" girl and a paraplegic guy "on the job". The stress is on being "creative". It's like you want to know, but you don't want to know . . . you know?'

'We could do other things.'

'I'm not an experiment.'

'That's a shitty thing to say.' I snatched up the bottle of champagne and took an angry swig. I felt drunk and unlovely. Why couldn't we have stayed kissing? I hadn't thought about the chair once while we were kissing.

Dylan drew circles in the dirt. He found his cigarettes and lit one. But he only took one puff before putting it out. I took another swig of champagne. I burped out, 'Dy-lan,' and passed him the bottle. He burped, 'Ril-ey.' We went back and forth until the bottle was drained. I lay down. I rolled onto my side and closed my eyes. Dylan lay down too and his hand found its way into my dress. He was drawing stars and planets on my skin. It felt dreamy. Suddenly he pressed right up against me. I felt the shock of his skin on mine. He kissed me, and I shivered, even though I was feeling hot all over. He whispered, 'I think I changed my mind.'

Later I would remember Dance with a Difference. The way the dancers would freeze in certain poses, and how my heart clenched in suspense. How long could they hold out? I could see them sweating, see their chests rise and fall. I searched their faces for a sign of surrender. I held my breath and trembled. When Dylan and I began we were deathly serious, like we were arranging ourselves. But there was slippage and stoppage, and that pesky condom business and silly sound effects. I'm glad it was Dylan who laughed first. Once he did I felt myself unravel. I giggled and he giggled. *We* were the experiment. And then there came a time when we weren't laughing. When we locked eyes and breathed each other's breath. Ohmystars! The firmament shakes and then everything settles. In the end everything settles.

ON THE SIXTH DAY

Everything Beautiful

I woke up in the desert with a dry mouth and Dylan's arm hooked around my waist. The air felt cool and every few seconds I'd hear a sound – a kind of *plink-plink* that could have been a dripping tap, or Bird's fabled Crimson Chat. I thought I didn't want to wake up. Dylan smelled like the lake. He was salt-stained. He had crystals in his eyelashes and stubble on his chin. I *thought* I didn't want to wake up but when I turned around I almost swooned. The lake was impossibly red and still, like a brilliant spill of paint. I disentangled myself and stared. This could not be real. It was too much. It was like an elaborate stage set. Any minute now the lid on the sky would close, and the roof of the minimall with all its dirty ducts and rigging would be revealed. And we, the Mutard mall-heads would go wow-wow-wow! And go back to shopping.

What was it about the desert that left me stumbling for words? Words were human tools – but this . . . this *vision* had nothing to do with us; it had occurred in spite of us. I felt like I was trespassing. I was a rude speck on an ancient tapestry. Then I felt grateful. I wasn't sure to whom – God or Buddha or the Big Bang – but while I stared, while there was no past or future, just the sky and the lake, I felt that I had been let in on some kind of Utopia. In a matter of minutes, as the sun continued to rise, the brilliance died – like everything beautiful had to.

I gathered some stones and bark and an iridescent green feather and arranged them in a pile at the foot of the monster gum – like a poem. Dylan woke up, checked his breath in his cupped hands and said, 'I don't suppose you brought toothpaste?'

Morning had broken.

SUCKINGFISH

'I think you should stay here,' I decided. 'It'll be quicker.'

'That's very chivalrous of you.' Dylan's voice had some sulk in it.

I sighed. 'What are you going to do – drag yourself?'

He folded his arms and faced me. 'I could.'

'Don't be stupid.' I was trying to pretend the prospect of chafing my way solo through the scrub was the realisation of a life-long dream, but I was generating sweat beads. I kept throwing hopeful glances at Delilah's tyre despite the fact that we couldn't have changed it if we tried. We had no tools, no jack, no clue.

'I'm hungry,' Dylan announced. He went through my bag pulling things out: the empty pack of biscuits, the water, my lighter, *Utopia*, my notebook, Neville's Jesus badge, toilet paper. Dylan held up two apples. He threw one to me and crunched into the other. He chewed noisily. 'Someone will come. Bird knows we're here. Olive knows we're here.'

'They won't say anything. They're weird like that.'

'What about Sarita?'

'I didn't tell her.'

Dylan pointed his apple at me and recited, 'The first thing you do before you go into the wild is tell a friend.'

'So who did you tell?'

'No one.' He sighed and twirled his apple by its stem. 'Someone will figure it out . . . won't they?'

I gave him a doubtful glance. 'You want to wait and find out?'

Dylan pushed his hands on his wheels, forward and back, forward and back. 'How long do you think it would take to walk to the Nhill road?'

'I don't know. At least an hour.'

'Do you know which way to go?'

'Well, it's the fire road . . . there are markers.' I paused. 'It's not *all* sand.'

Dylan took a big drink of water. He stretched his arms above his head, then brought them down and swung his elbows left and right. He rolled his shoulders, watching me all the while, and finally said, 'Let's go.'

'Are you sure?'

'When I get tired, you can push.' Dylan started off. 'You know, you can get wheelchairs for the beach. They have fatter tyres, better traction.'

'If you can walk with the crutches, why do you use the chair?'

'Have you ever had crutches?'

I shook my head. Dylan reached behind his chair for his crutches. I put them under my arms. I swung, landing with both feet on the dirt. 'It's not completely uncomfortable.'

'Next time keep your feet up.'

I tried. I couldn't. I felt it in my arms, and stomach. 'Oof! Ouch!'

Dylan held his arms out. I gave the crutches back.

Sometimes the ground was hard, and Dylan would mad-man it, ramming his hands down on his wheels, whooping as he went. When we faced another wide tract of sand, he'd go on the crutches and I'd push his empty chair. It was like taking one step forward and two steps back, and it was *fun*.

We'd been on the fire road for about half an hour when Dylan suddenly started laughing.

'What?'

He stopped, and wiped his eyes. 'I was just thinking this is like that footprints poem.'

I waited.

'You have to know the footprints poem – it's on a million tea-towels and fridge magnets. It's an industry in itself.'

I shook my head. 'I don't know it.'

Dylan said, 'Okay, it's like this person has died and he gets to meet God and he looks back over the steps of his life – like footprints on a beach – and there are two sets of footprints to show that God is with him. But then the guy notices that during the worst times of his life, there's only one set and he's like, "*Oh God, why did you abandon me?*"'

'No – wait,' I stopped him. 'I do know this. God says, "*I didn't abandon you – that was when I carried you.*"'

'Right.' Dylan looked at me. 'You're carrying me, Riley. This is pretty special.'

He had a glint in his eye, like he knew he'd said something corny. But I decided this was a defence mechanism. It was like he was giving the truth some padding. The moment *was* special. I knew it, he knew it.

'Here,' I gave him some water. 'You've got scurvy.'

This was the beginning of our olde-worlde mini-play. It was 1700. Australia hadn't even been discovered. We were sailing from England on the *Excelsior* when a tempest sent our vessel crashing on the rocks. I was Miranda Bigger-bottom, a fine lady; Dylan was Jack Filthy, a common sailor. We were the sole survivors. We couldn't stand each other and yet . . . we needed each other if we were going to make it. 'Oh, *fiddlesticks*!' I dabbed at my eyes with a dainty handkerchief. 'How *odious* it is without my snuff.'

Dylan lurched and growled and spat. '*Curses, woman! I'll give ye snuff!*' And so on and so forth.

After Miranda Biggerbottom and Jack Filthy had reduced us to a state of incoherence and random collapsibility, Dylan used the rest stops to read aloud from *Utopia* – like Laurence Olivier.

'*Pride,*' he orated, '*like a hellish serpent gliding through human hearts – or shall we say like a suckingfish that clings to the ship of state? – is always dragging us back and obstructing our progress –* '

He stopped reading and spoke normally. 'Actually, that's pretty cool.' He read some more to himself then asked me, 'Do you think pride is the "*beastly root of all evil*"?'

'I wouldn't know,' I joked. 'I don't have any.'

'You do. Pride is what makes you different. You're full of it. When I first saw you I thought, She doesn't give a shit. She's like a wild girl. Your clothes and your hair . . .'

'At Orientation?'

'You were gorgeous in your boredom.'

'I just thought you were weird,' I confessed.

'Aye! Blasted wench!' Dylan reverted to Jack Filthy and I collapsed in laughter again.

We were adapting to our landscape. Our clothes became customised. I'd detached the train of Rose's wedding dress and abandoned it by a grass tree. Dylan had ditched his bow-tie and unbuttoned so his pale chest was getting some rays. I liked seeing his cross glinting in the sun.

At noon – when the sun was so high we couldn't stand it and had to take shelter under a tree – Dylan pointed a crutch to the sky. 'This is the longest I've been outdoors since February 2. I have taken more steps today than I have in all the days since February 2 put together. I have heard the Boobook's call. And I've had sex.'

I laughed. 'We did, didn't we?'

Dylan stopped. The road was visible between the wattle trees. We pushed on. We didn't speak or look at each other. I felt a rush of excitement. I couldn't stop smiling – and I think for Dylan it must have been the same. When we reached the road I got down on all fours and kissed it.

'Yes! Saved!'

THE POO AND THE TUFT

Dylan stayed in his chair while I practised my hitchhiker poses: psycho hitcher, nympho hitcher, psycho hitcher. We shared the last cigarette. He ran a finger down my exposed back. 'You should use sunscreen,' he told me. Suddenly I saw us the way anyone passing (would there be anyone passing?) would see us. Two teenagers. One fat, one crippled, both bleary, in dead people's clothes.

I started laughing. 'We are so fucked.'

'What do you mean?'

'Look at us. Would you stop for us?'

'I'd stop for anyone.'

'You would, wouldn't you?'

Dylan smiled. I stuck my lip out. 'I'd stop for no one.'

I saw the car before I made the connection. I even saw their faces and it still didn't click. It was a problem of context. The black Monaro slowed and I chased after it. I shouted, 'Oh, thank God!' to the head hanging out the passenger window and then I heard the familiar cackle, and the girl pulled up her oversized sunglasses and screamed, 'Riley, what the fuck?' I looked past Chloe's head and saw Ben Sebatini – *the* Ben Sebatini – with his strong hands resting on the wheel.

He stopped the car. Chloe opened her door and stumbled clownishly out. She was in her silver party dress – the one that made her look like an Amazon from outer space – and her Yeti boots with the four-inch platforms. I was so happy to see her I reeled. I jigged up and down and backwards. 'What are you doing here? How is this possible?'

'Did you get *married*?' Chloe's eyes were black poker chips. Her skin had that E-sheen to it. She thumped me on the arm, once, twice. 'My friend, my friend, this is Fate – we were coming to get you! We left the party – ' She turned to Ben, 'What time did we leave the party?'

Ben lowered his seventies cop sunglasses. 'About eight.' He pushed them back up. He was chewing gum.

'He's *so* Starsky,' Chloe giggled. 'We've been driving for, like, ever.' She suddenly hugged her stomach. 'Oh my God. I have to go.'

She grabbed a pack of tissues from her purse and ran into the scrub. Ben lowered his sunglasses again. 'Nice dress.' He stroked his tuft, and I stifled the impulse to laugh out loud. I pictured their drive, doof-doof on the stereo, and the pair of them popping pills all the way.

'How was the party?' My voice came out oddly formal.

Ben moved his head up and down, to a beat only he could hear. 'Killer.'

I nodded. I didn't know what else to say. Ben Seb, my big crush. But. I didn't know how to talk to him. I wasn't comfortable with him. I realised I'd never even been sober around him.

'So . . . you came all the way to get me?'

Ben cricked his neck. 'You know how it gets. Gotta keep going forward. Like a shark.'

I was so glad Dylan hadn't heard that – it had sound bite all over it.

Chloe stumbled back. She shielded her eyes against the sun and pointed to Dylan. 'Who he?'

'That's Dylan.'

'Where'd you find the chair?'

'It's a *wheelchair*.'

'Oh.' Chloe looked again. '*Oh!*' She beamed at me. She touched my cheek. 'It's so good to see you.' They must have been some party pills. I was getting a contact high.

Chloe stroked my hair and stared at me and rambled. 'We passed a giant koala on the way. I wanted to get out but Ben was scared.'

'I wasn't scared!' Ben shouted from the driver's seat.

'You were.' She leant in and thumped him, then turned back to me. 'The koala's eyes were all yellow.'

I laughed. 'How gone are you?'

'Spaz! It's not a real koala. It's fibreglass. For tourists. You know, like the Big Banana, or the Giant Earthworm.' Chloe started dancing. She couldn't stay still. She clapped and wiggled like a wayward children's entertainer.

'Can you give us a lift back?' I asked.

'To Christian camp? My friend, my friend, I've been *dreaming* about it.'

'Okay, I'll get Dylan. Just . . .'

'What, what?'

'Be nice.'

Chloe was staring up at the sky. She laughed, 'I'm always nice. Look – ' She pointed. 'A daytime moon. I love a daytime moon.' She started doing a moondance, hailing the moon with her outstretched hands. My mind went back to Orientation, to the feverish Mallees and their wave of Praise. And Dylan with his head bowed, playing with his silver cross, thinking I was gorgeous.

Dylan!

I ran back to him. He was trying not to look anxious. Before he could say anything I said, 'This is so weird. I know them. It's Chloe . . . and Ben.'

'The tuft?'

'Shhh. Let's go.'

Chloe's eyes widened when she saw Dylan at close range – the suit, the hair, the chair – it was a devastating combo. 'Oh, wow.' I don't know why I was worried about her saying something awful. Chloe wasn't mean-spirited. She wasn't a starer or an avoider. She was just Chloe – spiky and surreal. She elbowed me. 'He's cute.' Dylan blushed.

Ben was less than subtle. He'd only been driving for two minutes when he looked at Dylan in the rear-view mirror. 'How'd you get like that?'

Dylan didn't blink. 'Drugs.'

'F-ark.' Ben's paranoia was a thing to behold. He eased off on the gas. He was doing *forty*.

'Why are you driving like an old person?' Chloe complained. Dylan's eyes slid left. He placed his finger under his nose, the tuftal region. We collapsed into giggles. Chloe laughed too – at a leaf or a line in the sky, something going on in her own mad head. Ben just drove.

A Different Movie

I made Ben stop before the arches. '*He hath made everything beautiful in his time . . .*' Chloe quoted in a prissy voice. She turned to the back and lisped, 'Itth true. He really hath.' Her face was blank as a doll's. Suddenly she shrilled, 'Wrong Way Go Back!' Dylan and I laughed. We were holding hands, surreptitiously, I thought, but Chloe clucked, 'Riley, you are a tart.' Concern flickered across her face. 'You're coming back with us, right?' She kept on. 'You have to see the koala. It's *evil*. I think you can go right into its head. Like, I think there are stairs all the way up. We'll have to stop on the way back and take photos.'

Dylan wriggled his shoulder into mine. I talked out of the corner of my mouth, like a hitman. 'How are we going to do this?'

He sliced the air with the palm of his hand. 'Just go straight in.'

'No. I mean *this*.' I squeezed his hand.

'Are you leaving right now?'

His question surprised me. Of course I was leaving.

Hadn't I been trying to leave since I first arrived? But then . . . things had changed.

'Not *right* now.' I waffled. 'No. I have to get my stuff . . .'

I felt confused. Being in Ben Seb's car was okay only because of Dylan and Chloe. Without Dylan I'd be the spare tyre. If Chloe fell asleep – and she had to crash sometime – then it would just be Ben and me and that would be awkward. Like being in a taxi. In taxis I always felt like I had to relate to the driver. I'd say, '*You must really like driving*' or '*I've heard those beaded seat covers are great.*' What did I have to talk to Ben about? Nothing. The more I tried to picture leaving with Chloe and Ben the less I could see it.

I said to Dylan, 'Is that bad? It's bad, isn't it? I'm leaving you with Neville – in the shit . . . holding the baby.'

Dylan smiled. 'I like the baby. It's our baby.'

Chloe interjected. 'You guys are so cute! You even argue cute.'

'We're not arguing,' Dylan and I said together.

The Monaro crawled up the drive. I stayed sitting, barely breathing, trying to work out what to do. Six days ago there would have been no question. Six days ago I would have clung to Ben's ride like that old suckingfish and never looked back. If I left now then I wouldn't have to witness Roslyn's everlovin' jumpsuit jamboree. I wouldn't have to suffer Anton's derision, or Neville's niceness. I wouldn't have to cut Fleur's hair. Or spin shit for the talent show. But I wouldn't get to farewell Sarita or Bird or Olive. Or Dylan Luck, whose face, I saw, had gone hospital green.

'Shit.' He pointed to a fish-stickered Tarago. 'That's Mum's car.' Next to the Tarago was Dad's Camry. I felt deflated. 'Oh, snap.'

Chloe tried to keep the vibe alive. She threw her arms up. 'Come on, party people. We'll drive west. We'll follow the sun. We've got pills – ' she poked Ben, 'haven't we? Let's just drive until we run out of petrol, see how far we get.'

But Dylan had already opened his door.

Ben cut the engine. Chloe blurted, 'It'll be like a movie!'

For a second I was with her. The sky was blue, the sun was infernal, the road was a gunmetal stripe in a red desert. Chloe would be sunbaking on the bonnet of the Monaro. But where was I? I couldn't see me.

Ah. I was in a *different* movie.

QUE SERA SERA

We all got out of the car. Ben was hovering around Dylan, but Dylan didn't need help. We watched him snap his chair into place, and transport himself into it. Ben was nodding, stroking his tuft, murmuring, 'Cool.'

Chloe patted Dylan's hand. 'Dylan, you have a feline grace.'

Dylan nodded. 'Chloe, you need to lie down.' He did a sly wheelie, and started for the path. Chloe was holding my hands, giving me her sympathetic shop girl smile. I broke away from her. 'Dylan, wait. I'm coming with you.'

Ben groaned. 'Make up your mind.'

'Shh,' Chloe smacked him. 'It's *romantic*.' Then she stamped her foot. 'I want to come too – Riley – at least let me explore?'

I hugged her tight. 'I'll see you back in the real world.'

'Are you sure? Your dad is going to be feral.'

I dug in my bag and found the Jesus badge. 'Here,' I pressed it into her palm. Chloe looked down and giggled. 'Oh man. That's beautiful. That's me.' She pinned the badge on her dress and shimmied. '*Church girl Fresh!*'

'Thanks for the lift,' I called to Ben.

He waved. 'We came, we saw, we went away.' He looked at me, but his expression was vague. And then he looked at Chloe and I saw hunger in his eyes. Hunger and pseudo-ephedrine and the possibility of a tumble. Did he even like me? Did I even care? The answer to both questions was No.

Ben beckoned to Chloe who had started to moondance again. 'Bitch! Hustle. We've got company.'

Craig was marching up the path. He did not look happy. He walked past Chloe without so much as an eyebrow hike and came straight for me.

'You're dead.' He grabbed my shoulder. I was too surprised to squeak.

'Hey – get off her.' Chloe bristled. 'You big . . . lug.'

Craig blanked her and said to me, 'Dylan could have died out there.'

I managed to snap, 'Does he look dead to you?'

Dylan looked decidedly alive. His hair was scruffy and his face was sunburnt and he was wearing half a suit, but his eyes were clear and his pose was absolutely open.

Craig shook me harder. 'You fat bitch! You're crazy.'

'Whoa!' Chloe held her hand up. 'I'm not hearing this.'

And while I was trying to process it all, Dylan rammed his chair into Craig's legs. Craig buckled. 'Dude – what the?'

'Don't talk to Riley like that.'

Craig stared at him. His face was all twisted with hurt.

'This is ugly.' Chloe rubbed her temples and nodded in Craig's direction. 'I'm getting a bad reading. I think he might be *evil*.' Chloe was mystical on E. Everything meant something. Life was black or white. Her gut didn't speak, it roared.

Ben had started backing out. 'Let's GO!' The passenger door was swinging. Chloe gave me a sweet smile, a *que sera sera*. She tromped after the Monaro and managed to jump in. Soon they were dust, and then they were nothing. I turned back to the camp. Craig was leaning on the Tarago, rubbing his shin, glowering. Neville had come out of his office. My dad was there, and Norma. In a weird way, I felt relieved to see them. They signified home. Norma was wearing her white linen ass-pants – the ones Chloe and I always laughed over because really, they were thong-fodder, but Norma would never go there. I chanced a smile and got stony faces in return. I tugged at Rose's wedding dress, tried to salvage the gaping back. Blah.

A dark-haired woman was standing next to Neville – crying silently.

Dylan wheeled up to her. He touched her gently on the arm. 'Mum – I want you to meet someone. This is Riley Rose. It's okay, we're not married.' He turned to give me a beautiful smile. 'We're just in deep like.'

THE GIRL I WAS

The first thing they did was separate us. Neville took Dylan
and his mother into his office, and I stayed outside with
Dad and Norma. They stood around me with their heads
and arms hanging limply. I moved over to the picnic bench –
the one that Norma and I had sat on that first day, a hundred
years ago. Norma patted her permanent. For once she let
Dad take the lead. He didn't *want* to be angry but his face
had become a tribal war mask. And when he spoke he
couldn't control his levels.

'What were you thinking? What were you THINKING?
You took a crippled boy off camp property. OVERNIGHT!
You stole a car, Riley. My daughter, a car thief! Did
you see that boy's mother? She's talking about a LAWSUIT.
And I'm not even going to talk about how worried we
were.'

'I wish you would,' I muttered.

Dad leaned in. 'What was THAT?'

'I wish you would. I'd like to hear it.'

Dad fumbled and his anger fizzled. He never was very

good at confrontation. 'Well, of course we were worried. But now you're back, and you look okay – ' He paused to look me over. 'Are you okay?'

I nodded.

'Right. So now that we know you're okay, well, I'm just furious.' But he didn't sound it anymore. He'd been defused. 'Furious,' he started again, with a bit more wind up. He looked to Norma as if she were feeding him lines and added, 'And disappointed. And embarrassed.'

'Well, I'm sorry,' I said. 'I'm sorry I'm such an embarrassment to you. But you've seen this place – what did you think was going to happen? Did you think you could tame me? I'm a wild girl! I'm all Grrr!' I growled and clawed the air.

Norma stepped forward. She put her hand up like a conductor trying to ease in the strings. 'Riley. Do you think you're transposing some of your anger at us onto the world at large? Do you think that we – your father in particular – deserve a little more respect and perhaps even an explanation?'

I stopped and thought about it. 'Yes. But.' My mouth stayed open – an avalanche was coming. Then: 'Dylan came of his own free will. We were looking for the salt lake – it's supposed to have healing properties. I was trying to help him. I even did a petition. My friends Olive and Bird helped us. We went into the desert and had to *walk* back. But it's beautiful there. When the sun rose over the salt lake it looked like the end of the world. It's supposed to be a desert but it's full of stuff. Wildflowers and birds – you should see their colours – like paint store swatches – only better because they're real.'

'Well – 'Norma started and couldn't finish.

'Did you say you had friends?' Dad asked.

'Yes, Olive and Bird. And Sarita as well. She's my roommate – she's mad – only you wouldn't know straight up. She's like those chocolate clinkers that you bite into and you never know what colour you're going to get.'

Dad and Norma looked at each other.

Norma said, 'So . . . you've had fun here?'

I shrugged. 'Sort of.' I thought about Dylan and felt panic brewing. 'Maybe if I talk to Dylan's mum, she'll calm down and see I was trying to do a good thing.'

Dad squinted towards the office. 'Let's not worry about that just yet.'

'Maybe if I tell her Dylan doesn't need to be cured because there's nothing wrong with him. He's perfect.' And then suddenly I was *crying*. Real Life Actual Tears were sliding down my face and making my skin sting. They tasted like the salt lake. I cried and coughed and spluttered. And I couldn't stop. I was a mess. Maybe I was transposing now. These tears weren't about my Spirit Ranch Shenanigans, they were for Mum and Dad and me. I felt my father's arms enfold me and free up a whole other vat of tears. I cried like a girl, a big fat girl. The girl I was.

END OF FAITH DISCUSSION

There was only one path to Neville's office. I heard his door open and gathered myself and tried not to look like such a trainwreck. I wriggled out from under Dad's arm. I didn't want Dylan to think I'd gone soft. When they came out, Dylan's mum was pushing his wheelchair. He was holding his MP3, untangling his earplugs. His mum didn't look at me, or Dad or Norma. She had dark sunglasses and a mouth like a prune. She looked like she was waiting for the tabloids to descend with flashbulbs and microphones, like this really was a courtroom drama. And now it was my turn to give evidence, to plead guilty.

Your honour, I admit it. I didn't think about afterwards . . .

Dylan's eyes flicked up. He gave me his casual-drug-dealer nod, but the spark wasn't behind it, and that made me worry. I told myself that things were going to be okay. Soon – maybe even after lunch – we would be alone again. Free to roll our eyes and make our jokes and work some more on our trust games. I held my hand out to my side, discreet as I could be. As he passed, we linked pinkies and that second confirmed everything. That second would sustain me through-out Neville's lecture. Once that was done we could get back to normal. That's what I was thinking: Grade Three logic.

Neville looked like he'd just discovered Roslyn running a numbers racket out of the counsellors' annexe. He addressed Dad and Norma. 'If it's all right with you I'd like to talk to Riley alone.'

'Oh, well – ' Dad started to protest but Norma elbowed him.

'That's fine, Neville.'

It wasn't fine with me. I actually felt a little scared. You hear stories about mild-mannered types who reach their stress capacity and go postal. Psychos always have names like Neville, and mother issues, and weird weapons collections. What if he stabbed me with his Jesus badges?

Neville held the door open for me. I slunk in and sat in the squeaky chair and he sat opposite me in his authoritarian throne. He had one of those Newton's Cradles – the silver balls strung up that go clackety-clack-infinity. I lifted one. I watched the balls go back and forth. I could have watched them forever. I guess that's the point.

'Riley Rose.' Call me The Plague. A small smile twitched on Neville's lips. He spoke mystically – someone had put Yoda in his tea: 'Things run smoothly for so long that you can't even imagine it any other way – and then one act makes everything stop.' Neville put his finger in between the silver balls and killed the flow. The absence of noise made my palms sweat. I wiped them on Rose's dress, which was a shambles.

'Let's talk facts. Fraser's car – I understand you left it in the desert?'

I nodded silently.

'It's missing a wheel? Last time I looked it didn't even have wheels.'

I stared straight ahead. I wasn't about to dob on Bird.

Neville studied my face as if searching for cracks. 'Must have been the car fairy. Do you know the location of the car?'

'Near the salt lake.'

'Near the salt lake,' Neville nodded. 'Facts. There was a bottle of champagne in the counsellors' fridge that's gone walkabout. Do you know anything about that?'

Ditto Olive. 'I took it.'

'You managed to coerce Dylan into "escaping"?'

'Yes.' I didn't know what Dylan had told him, but if taking the blame meant Bird and Olive and Dylan stayed shiny happy in Neville's head then that's what I would do.

Neville straightened random items on his desk. He frowned and spoke without looking at me. 'I was like you once: sullen, anti-social . . . It might surprise you to know that I used to be an atheist.'

That did surprise me, but I didn't say so. Neville clasped his hands together and looked up. Both eyes – even the glass one – stayed on me, unswerving, unnerving.

'When I was at university I had no faith. I considered myself to be free. Because if you are under someone else's authority then you are not free – and what is God if not authority? But then I worked out: we need rules. From the time we are children we need and respond to rules. We need to be governed. That's what makes us civilised.'

'Maybe we're not meant to be civilised,' I offered. 'Cavemen weren't.'

'How many cavemen do you know?'

'I can think of a few.'

'Mmm.' Neville paused. 'Think of it like this: the world is a picture and God is the frame. God is the structure. He's given us all this . . . and we have to . . . work together to fulfil his design. Riley, I can't make you believe what I believe but I know you'd be happier with a little faith.'

'I have faith. In some things.' In Dylan. I had faith in Dylan. And anyway, frames and structures were different things.

'Do you think you're the same girl who sat here six days ago?'

I folded my arms and said with a small smile, 'Pretty much.'

But my mind stormed. *Nooo!* I *had* changed. But it wasn't anything to do with God. It would have happened even if I hadn't come here. I went into a parallel universe – the one where Dylan and I stayed in the desert, searching for grub, dipping in the soaks, re-enacting *Utopia* at sundown, kissing and tumbling indefinitely.

'End of faith discussion.' Neville flexed and gave his desk a little love pat. 'What should I do – what course of action would be appropriate?'

I said in a small voice, 'Send me home?'

'Yes, but *what would you have learnt?*' Neville's mouth turned up. I looked at his chest and clocked his badge: *Jesus is coming . . . Look Busy.* I wanted to scowl but I couldn't. It was impossible to hate Neville.

'Dylan's going home,' Neville said. 'His mother is taking him home. He doesn't have a choice. You, however, have a choice.'

Dylan's going home. The words spun around my head like little evil planets.

'Think about it,' Neville said.

I walked out and Dad and Norma went in. I waited for them on the picnic bench. I sat in the bright sunlight swinging my feet and watching the shadows dance across the dust. I felt hazy, like I was coming down. I had been expecting Neville to lose it. I think I wanted him to be horrible to me so I could be horrible back. Instead he'd given me options. I could be at home without Dylan, or here without Dylan. At least here I had unfinished business. His mum's Tarago was still in the car park. Once upon a time I might have slashed the tyres or stuffed a banana in the exhaust pipe to keep him from leaving. Now I could hold my breath and still let him go.

Dad and Norma came back out. Norma was wearing a tight smile to match her ass-pants. Dad's smile was looser, fonder. He put his arm around my shoulder. 'Come on, Potato-head. Let's get your things.' And I opened my mouth and said the words he never thought he'd hear. 'I want to stay.'

And so it was decreed that Dad and Norma would spend the night at the Nhill B&B – a thrilling prospect by anyone's standards. Before getting in the Camry, Dad took me aside. 'What about this talent show?'

'Bring a book,' I advised him.

'Are you going to perform?'

'I'm going to do *something*. But I don't know what.'

'You know what your mother would have – '

'I'm *not* doing Ophelia.'

Dad's face went fuzzy. 'I wish she could be here to see you.'

'Maybe she is.'

THIS WAY UTOPIA

Dylan's mother stood outside his door like a bouncer. She had his bags at her feet. I paused at the end of the ramp to take a breath, and then I went for it. She tried to block me. I dodged from side to side. 'Can I say goodbye to Dylan?'

'You just go back.' She held her hand up. She could have pushed me – I'm guessing she wanted to. Her hand was as pale as Dylan's. I don't know why I did it, but I reached for it. I turned it over and stared at her palm.

'Your love-line is fine,' I told her. 'It's good and clean. And your lifeline is long. I'm an expert in this.' Dylan's mother didn't take her hand back. She let me hold it. I saw a tear escape her sunglasses. 'I'm really sorry,' I said quickly, without looking up. And then she just moved aside, like a spook on the ghost train. One minute she was in my face and the next she was gone.

Dylan was leafing through the camp program.

'Oh hi,' he said, super-casually. 'How are you?'

'Eh.' I sat down on the bed. 'Your mum is crying.'

'Surprise, surprise.' Dylan gave me a look of mock-reproach. 'What did you say to her?'

'I apologised.'

'What for?'

'Leading you astray . . . '

'You didn't.'

'I must have done something wrong,' I said. 'I feel awful.'

'Catholic guilt.'

'Minus the Catholic.'

Dylan wheeled over so his knees were knocking against mine. He held my hands and whispered, 'Don't feel bad. I had the best time ever.'

'Why are you whispering?' I smiled teasingly, and waited. And waited. I wanted him to kiss me. Where was my kiss?

'Will you sign my program?' Dylan asked in a big nerd voice.

'Oh. Okay.' I opened the map page and marked a big X where Fraser's house was located. I drew an arrow going into the desert and wrote: *This Way Utopia*. Then I wrote down my address, email and phone number, signed Miranda Biggerbottom.

Dylan crooked his finger at me. 'Come here.'

I leaned in.

'Closer,' he said.

I moved closer.

'Now, close your eyes.'

I closed my eyes. I smiled and waited. *Still* no kiss. I felt something else though, something light on the crown of my head, then it was falling down, fine as a spider web.

'Open your eyes,' Dylan told me.

I looked down to see his silver cross glinting in the hollow of my breastbone.

I frowned at it, unsure for a moment.

'I fully expect you to wear it upside-down,' Dylan mumbled. 'I just wanted to give you something. I've never taken it off before.' He touched his neck, patted the place where his cross used to be, and then he cleared his throat. 'Ahem.'

He put his hand on my face, tilted it slightly, smiled, and drew me in for a long frozen moment that grew into an earth-moving, stars-falling, sea-foam-smashing-on-the-rocks, slow-derangement-of-the-senses soul kiss.

We came up for air. He pressed his forehead against mine.

'Keep your eyes closed,' he whispered. I heard him pause and take a breath. His hands brushed his wheels and his chair creaked. I heard him push back and forward and finally, out. When I opened my eyes, the room was bright and Dylan had gone.

HOOTENANNY

I found Olive and Bird in the rec room. She was reading a book about the constellations; he was reading one of Fraser's notebooks.

'Delilah's gone,' I told them. 'So has Dylan.'

I sat down with the weird siblings and pressed my head into the sofa. They didn't ask me anything. Sitting between them was as good as a hug.

One by one the Honeyeaters trickled in from the mess hall. When Sarita saw me she came running up. She had glitter on her eyelids, and a smile to match.

'Oh Riley!' She clasped my hands and squeezed them. 'I thought perhaps you were never coming back. I said to Fleur that you were like a sunset: iridescent and inimitable and then . . . gone. And all that is left is the impression of greatness.' She gave me a trembly smile and then threw her head back and laughed like a maniac.

I blinked. 'Wow.'

'You like that?'

I nodded.

'I was acting. I have been practising my oratorical skills. I'm going to be the Master of Ceremonies for the talent show.'

'You sounded like a prophet.'

She punched the air. 'Yes!'

'What did Fleur say?

Sarita shrugged. 'She bitched about her hair.'

Roslyn walked in with a clipboard in her hand, her hair pulled back so tight it was like an instant facelift. She scanned the campers, found my face. She looked puzzled for a moment but then returned to form.

'Campers, listen up. You have some free time before dinner. I suggest you use it to master your acts for the talent show. There's no dress rehearsal, kids. Tomorrow is it, the big enchilada. Floor Managers, I want to see your running-sheets before we go in for dinner. Costumes, props, lights, music cues, all of it on paper.' Her voice rose above the chatter. 'If it's not on paper, it's not happening.'

The Honeyeaters swooped down on Sarita and chirped in her ear and stuck her with their beaks and scratched on her clipboard with their talons. Lisa and Laura were on the small stage, practising their steps to no music.

'What's the song?' I asked Sarita, pointing to them.

She checked her clipboard. '"Hot Legs" by Rod Stewart.'

'That's *so* wrong!'

Step, kick, head back, crump, crump, squat legs, jump, out, windmill, windmill, boom! They ended back to back, facing the world with cruel pouts.

The rec room looked like a hootenanny. Craig and Fleur were in a corner working on their harmony. He sang with his eyes closed but she stared straight at him as her voice wavered and quavered all over the place. In another corner Richard and Ethan were going through their Jesus Rap.

'Yo, yo, yo, Christ is the Man and I love him So (so)
He's the dude with the answers dontcha Know (know)'

Bird saw me looking and smiled. 'I don't need to practise,' he said.

'Me either.'

And then Roslyn was there, giving me a sisterly smile. 'Riley, I'm looking forward to your piece.'

Sarita said, 'I don't even have you scheduled!'

'That's okay,' I said. 'I don't have to – '

Roslyn spoke over me. 'Riley can close the show.'

'Oh, awesome.'

'So,' she pursed her lips. 'What have you got?'

I had Nothing. Roslyn was waiting for me, I could practically see her stress levels escalating. Her eyes dipped slightly. Her palm tree quivered. Just then Fleur came up. I never thought I'd be so happy to see her. She slunk her arm through mine. 'Sorry, Roslyn. Riley and I need to discuss hair and make-up. I'll give her back, I promise.'

THE APPEAL OF WRONGNESS

Fleur was sitting on the chair in front of me, looking like she wanted to change her mind. 'Be afraid,' I whispered, 'be very afraid.' I snipped the air with my scissors and cackled evilly.

Fleur frowned. 'You're so unprofessional.'

'I have scissors,' I deadpanned. 'So what kind of look do you want?'

'I don't want a *look*,' Fleur said. 'Just a trim, maybe a fringe.'

'Bo-ring.' I sighed and started combing her wet hair. I combed it into a palm tree, like Roslyn's, then a faux-hawk, like Craig's. I considered revenge.

On one nature walk, Anton had pointed out an Aboriginal 'canoe tree' – a red gum with a big scar down its trunk; long ago the missing bark had been used to shape a crude canoe. If I'd wanted to be really, *really* mean I could have given Fleur a canoe tree cut – perfect at the front, hacked-into at the back, the kind of cut that would leave people whispering in her wake. But revenge no longer seemed important. What did seem important was this: I could make Fleur look better, if only she'd let me.

A straight fringe is impossible with paper scissors and Fleur couldn't sit still. She kept faffing her hands around her crown – and making nervous noises – 'Don't go too short!'

As with Sarita's treatment, I had the chair facing the wall opposite the mirror. It was killing Fleur to know that all she had to do was turn, turn, turn and she'd see . . . the damage. I pictured myself spinning her around. Fleur – meet Raggedy Ann. Her scream would strip the stucco walls.

'As your hairdresser I advise you stop jiggling about.'

Fleur minced at me. She picked her nails and pouted.

'Can I ask you something?'

I stopped cutting. 'Okay.'

'Did you have sex with Craig?'

I was glad I was the one holding the scissors.

'No.'

'Oh.'

The conversation might have ended there but I heard myself saying, 'We were going to but he didn't want to use a condom.'

Fleur frowned. 'You knew he was with me, right? So what – you just don't like me?'

'I don't *dis*like you.'

'Was it the fat jokes?'

'I probably would have done it anyway.'

'Is that like Sir Edmund Hillary saying the reason he climbed Mount Everest was 'cause it was there?'

'A bit.' I wasn't about to broadcast my low self-esteem to the one person who wouldn't get it. Craig made me feel good. No. The *idea* of Craig made me feel good. How could

I explain the appeal of wrongness? Chloe always says 'never apologise, never explain' but I opened my mouth and –

'I'm sorry.' My apology hung in the air with the hair mist. I resumed cutting, but I was only making things worse. My hands were like lumps. I couldn't seem to cut straight.

Out of the blue, Fleur said, 'I don't think Craig actually *likes* me. I mean, I've been *saving* myself for him and he doesn't even seem to . . . ' She stopped. She looked like she was about to cry. 'I try to talk to him. Like, I think about it so hard. I write down the questions beforehand and I rehearse and then I ring him and read them out – and I never get any closer to knowing him. Do you think I should just have sex with him?'

'No!' I laughed. Then I looked at her hand gripping the edge of the sarong. This was serious business for Fleur. 'Maybe you should wait,' I suggested. 'Maybe there's someone better . . . you know, out there in the real world.'

'What if sex is the only way you get close to people?'

I didn't say anything.

'Tell anyone I said that and you die.' Fleur groaned. 'God. You lured me into your chair just to get me to spill. It's totally true about hairdressers being like therapists.'

'Fleur. I think you should go short.'

'Sell it to me.'

'I'm thinking something classic, simple, elegant. Think Audrey Hepburn. Think Natalie Portman. Think Winona Ryder post Johnny Depp, pre people's court.'

'Did you fuck it up?'

'I can fix it,' I assured her. 'Trust me.'

And she did. And I did.

ON THE SEVENTH DAY

Sir Thomas More's Prayer for the Maybes

On the seventh day there was no rest. No sooner had we woken up and showered and breakfasted than the parental units began to arrive. They stood around in awkward bunches. Fathers clapped other fathers on the back; mothers did that point-and-squeal thing that I know my mum *never* would have done. And every time I saw a counsellor I was reminded of fairground laughing clowns, like, are they laughing or are they *screaming*?

I picked out Olive and Bird's parents as soon as they walked into the rec room. They were both small and dark and intense. I took the introductions upon myself.

'Your son told me there's over two hundred birds indigenous to the Little Desert,' I said. 'I've started my list. I'm only up to three. I've got a long way to go.'

'Are you a Youth Leader?' their mother asked. She seemed amazed that anyone had connected with her offspring.

'God, no!' I laughed. 'I'm the Camp Sceptic.'

'Oh!' And now she smiled. 'How nice to meet you!'

There's nothing more telling than parents. Craig's father was a military man. His uniform was as stiff as his expression. He looked like he had a cement pylon shoved up his arse. He barked questions at his son, and then cut over the answers. Craig scratched at his neck every time his father addressed him. I even heard him *stammer*.

Fleur's mother was wearing top-to-toe Laura Ashley and white gloves, like some society matron, but she was a spit-talker and when she laughed it sounded like a cat-fight.

I was leaning by the door, thinking about how Dad and Norma almost seemed normal, when Sarita grabbed my hand. 'You must meet my parents.'

'Really?'

Sarita's mother was beautiful, but sad. She looked like she'd seen the sky fall. Her father just looked grey. Poor Sarita. She squeezed my hand and bubbled with new confidence. 'This is Riley Rose – she is my mentor. The star that lights the southern sky!' Her parents didn't give any indication that they'd even heard her. Sarita sighed. She turned to me with her eyes flashing boldly. 'The fuck of it is I'm all they've got.' Then she pinched my arm. 'Fffff! It feels so good to finally say it!'

Roslyn kicked off the talent show by bugling 'How Great Thou Art'. I sat through the program and let myself be swept away by the jerry-built beauty of it all – the hyper-kinetic Bronzewings and the manic Mallees and the heartfelt Honeyeaters – all trying so hard to please. The parents applauded politely and trapped their yawns behind cupped palms. Time crawled. Richard and Ethan rapped. Sarita's MC style was smooth and insinuating. I predicted a career in television journalism. I thought about Dylan. I'd heard for last year's talent show he'd put on a magic show. He had put Fleur in a box and sawn her in half while she squealed with laughter. I pictured him up there, sawing away, owning the stage. I thought about how for his mother that was probably the picture of the way she wished he could be. But I liked the new Dylan. I closed my eyes and wanted him next to me.

And then Roslyn was hissing at me. 'You're on!'

Sarita hailed me as I walked onto the stage. I saw my father beam with pride.

The room fell silent. I looked at all the certain and expectant faces. I wanted to tell them that the God thing was imposs but instead I took *Utopia* out of my bag and opened up to the back of the book and read Sir Thomas More's prayer for the Maybes.

Oh God, I acknowledge Thee to be my creator, my governor, and the source of all good things. I thank Thee for all Thy blessings, but especially for letting me live in the happiest possible society, and practise what I hope is the truest religion. If I am wrong, and if some other religion or social system would be better and more acceptable to Thee, I pray Thee in Thy goodness to let me know it, for I am ready to follow wherever Thou shalt lead me. But if our system is indeed the best, and my religion the truest, then keep me faithful to both

of them, and bring the rest of humanity to adopt the same
way of life, and the same religious faith – unless the present
variety of creeds is Thy inscrutable purpose.

I stopped there, because it was only going to get fruitier. The audience clapped – slowly at first – then louder and louder. I saw my father clapping so hard his hands must have hurt. I heard my mother saying, 'Jay-sus!' Everyone sang 'Amazing Grace' in various strains of dodgy disharmony. And I didn't feel like a wretch, and I didn't feel saved but maybe no one else did either, maybe they were just singing. Maybe it was the being together that counted.

After the group photo I was back on the smokers' bench – alone. I wasn't smoking. I was just sitting. The clouds in the sky looked all bundled up, like a mummy, or a roast, or a fat girl in a mesh vest. I was thinking about *Survivor* – the TV show – how week after week the contestants drop off until it's down to two – and then the final two have to do this so-called spiritual walk where they go back to their old camp and revisit each of the old contestants. The final two fake reverence. They drop fond comments: '*Oh, yeah, Taneka was really strong.*' Or they quote the contestants: '*No way am I eating that witchetty grub, dude!*'

Sitting on the bench I had something of that final survivor feeling. I visited the sites in my mind: the river, the crater, the roundabout, Dylan's cabin, Fraser's house. I saw Fleur's first snarl, and Bird's creeping blush. I saw Sarita whirling around in my mother's necklace, and Richard and

Ethan chanting to God. I saw Olive scrubbing away in the kitchen, her mind somewhere infinitely more exciting, and I saw Roslyn holding her little green book in both palms like it contained the answer to everything.

Roslyn's thought for the morning had been: *Go on knocking and it shall be opened unto you.* I closed my eyes and pictured the world and all its hinges. It was open, just a crack. There was a thin sliver of light. I could almost touch it.

Manifesto Revised

I believe in Chloe and friendship and love now.
I will always think of Dylan when I hear the Boobook owl.
I believe most girls are insecure and most guys are bluffing.
I believe the more you spill, the messier you get.
I don't believe in miracles but I do believe in spirits.
I believe there are more questions than answers.
I believe the best part is still to come.
(I still believe in chocolate!)

Acknowledgements

I would like to give big thanks to Anna McFarlane, Mary Verney, Sue Bobbermein, Melanie Cecka, Sarah Odedina, Jill Grinberg and Fran Bryson for all their smart stuff; country roses to my family and friends who put up with me nicking their stories and dodging their phone calls; excellent scotch to Alana Lucas and Campbell Message for tech support in all things 'Mutard'; Tiffany glass to Melita Granger who believed in Riley from the first; and everything beautiful to Mark and Willeford, who keep life sweet.

I wrote *Everything Beautiful* at Glenfern, an old St Kilda manse-turned-writers' retreat. Without it my book would be half-written and covered in Play-Doh. Many thanks to Joel Becker, Iola Matthews and the Victorian Writers' Centre for the residency, and to the writers with whom I shared cups of tea and word counts.

SOURCES

Utopia by Sir Thomas More, 1516; The little green book that Roslyn reads from is *God Who Created Me*, including the poem 'Each in His Own Tongue' by W Carruth; *The Mansions of Space* by John Morressy (1983); Riley's fable about the 'Owls of Athens' comes from an episode of the UK children's television show, *Bagapuss* (1974); *Footprints* is by Mary Stevenson (1936). Thanks to Colin Thiele, and Joselyn Burt's *The Little Desert* (1975) for inspiration.

By the same author

Simmone Howell is an award-winning short-story writer, and screenwriter. Her short film *Pity24* won an AWGIE award and has screened at film festivals such as the London Australian Film Festival and Los Angeles Shorts Fest. Her first novel, *Notes from the Teenage Underground*, won the Victorian Premier's Literary Award for Young Adult Fiction in 2007. Visit: www.simmonehowell.com